Printed in the United States of America.

For licensing/copyright information, additional copies or for use in specialized settings contact:

James Colwell

412-322-6464

www.JCNovels.com

Email: jcnovels@msn.com

Between Pews

A novella by James Colwell

This book is dedicated to all those
who have turned to the church in
search of safety and fellowship, but
once you arrived all you discovered
was
full-o-sh**

James Colwell

Between Pews

Table of Contents

"Standing In Your Truth"

Chapter One

"Welcome To The Burgh"

My name is Edwin James and I am
originally from the Baltimore, Maryland
area. I am a freelance journalist and have
done very well for myself in the past twelve
years. I have been offered a management
position with a new magazine in the
Pennsylvania area. It's been two months
since I moved to Pittsburgh and I've met a
couple of folks, but the one person that
stands out is my downstairs neighbor
Miranda. She is a bit of a spit-fire; she's
26 years old with no children and a decent

job. Miranda is about 5 foot 6 inches tall, has a small waist and good tits. She is very pleasant to the eye and has a personality to match. She has the spirit of the outgoing; on the first day I moved into this apartment building she came right up to the door and introduced herself while the movers were carrying my things in. I could tell that she was sniffing; all that testosterone tapped into the bloodhound in her and brought her running, she carefully scanned and sized up each of the movers and me. Let's just say my friend Miranda knows what she's likes and understands what she's working with and she considers herself young, free, single and more than ready to mingle. As I ran out later that evening to grab a few groceries I noticed one of the moving trucks had returned, I looked around for a moment and didn't see any of the movers so I continued on to the store and thought no more about it. When I came back in and passed Miranda's door on the first floor I couldn't miss the great time that was being had by her and the owner of an extremely deep voice. I won't lie, I got

pretty tickled and stood there in the hall
for a moment and listened as my neighbor
instructed her guest to dig her out, with
warning of an oncoming explosion. I shook
my head, laughed and ran up the stairs and
proceeded to my apartment saying to myself,
'Must be nice!' The next morning as I was
leaving for work I again noticed the moving
van still in it's same spot. I sat in my
car for a moment checking to make sure that
I had all the documents in my briefcase that
I needed for the day ahead. As I wrapped up
my things with the satisfaction that I was
all set, I closed my briefcase, placed my
seatbelt in place and just as I went to pull
out from my parking space, out of the front
door of the apartment complex walked a
chocolate covered Adonis. He stood about 6
foot, 3 inches tall with bowed legs and a
washboard stomach; he wore 5 thick cornrows
to the back of his head without a strand of
hair out of place. Every feature in his
face looked as if it were chiseled by an
artist. I tried not to stare, but it was a
little hard to do; within seconds he was
walking directly in front of my vehicle, he

looked directly into my face and as his left
eyebrow raised we both recognized each
other; he was definitely one of the movers
that came in to move my things the day
before. He walked around to my window; as I
rolled it down, his deep voice rang out,
"Good morning man," he extended his hand for
a shake. And I obliged, I immediately
became a little flustered at the strength of
his grip. I replied, "Wassup," while trying
to keep the eye contact at the eye; my
goodness what a struggle that was. He said,
"It feels great out here this morning. Your
first name was Ed or Edward right?" I said,
"Almost, it's Edwin - Edwin James, and thank
you for the great job you guys did moving me
in yesterday; everything went very smoothly,
I appreciate that." He responded, "Sorry
bought that Mr. James, I'm bad with names
sometimes, I'm glad you used our company to
move you. My name is Rafik Jerry, and you
were about the easiest client that I've ever
dealt with for the whole three years I've
been doing this job. Usually people are
real picky and fussy and hanging all over
the movers to the point that we can't get

our work done. And you have some real nice shit," he dropped his head in embarrassment, then continued, "Excuse me, I'm working on my mouth." I thought immediately to myself, 'I can definitely help you out with that!' I laughed out loud and said, "Don't worry about it Rafik, and you can call me Ed." I then noticed that he had not let go of my hand and the handshake was well over with. He said, "Cool, you're new here right!" I replied, "Yup, I am." He said, "Cool, maybe we can hook up and I can show you some sights. I don't live very far from here, I live right over on the West End, I can get over here to the Northside in a matter of minutes." I said, "That's nice of you, I guess I will have to take you up on that. I'm surprised though, what were you doing in Maryland?" He laughed and said, "Didn't you notice the last name on the moving company, Jerry's Moving. There are two Mr. Jerrys, one is my dad and the other is my uncle. I float back and forth, my family is here in Pittsburgh and my uncle's family is in Maryland. My dad runs this end and his bro runs that end. Me and four of my cousins split up our time between the two places, it's cheap to do it that way, because we can stay with family and it doesn't cost the company anything. Funny thing is, it's not often that I get the trip from the Baltimore area to Pittsburgh, it's usually the other way around." I said, "I'll bet; but I was offered a job that I couldn't refuse. I can go home to party if I can't find somewhere to party around here in this quiet little town." He said, "Ah, watch it, it's not all that quiet, we gotta hook up playboy! I'ma let you get off to work," he finally let my hand go and reached in his pocket for his cellphone and said, "Ed J. gimme your digits and I'll hit you up later." I laughed and said, "Ed J." He smiled a smile that damn near blinded me coupled with the sun and said, "Yeah, I like that for you, it fits you, with your soft ass hands and shit." I acted as if I didn't notice that last part of the comment, as I put my cellphone number in the phone. I knew right away that Mr. Rafik Jerry had picked up on the fact that I bat for the other team. And I wasn't 100% sure but I was pretty convinced that he was batting for both teams. I handed the phone back to him, he took it and locked my name and number in. He flashed that damn smile again and said, "I'ma hit you up later, aight." I smiled and said, "Okay, that's cool." As he turned to walk away, I lustfully took in the sight of all that he had to offer. I told myself, 'Don't put too much into that, he has already shown that he is a sexually charged free agent, and that can be the opening for a lot of confusion, which I can't stand.'

That first day at work literally got started two minutes after I stepped in the door and was reacquainted with the folks in the office. I hadn't been given a whole lot of time with folks I'd be managing at the magazine. The nice thing about my job is I would be managing a group of writers, some freelance and some were actually on staff with the magazine. With that, it allowed me a steady paycheck and the opportunity to work from home and in the field(which opened the door for travel, hallelujah). I could continue writing novels on the side as well; I was very happy with my current circumstances. The only thing was the move, I absolutely did not want to move to Pittsburgh; in Baltimore there was always something going on, so I could constantly have something published in several publications in the area, this was going to be a bit of a stretch in this calm, family oriented area.

After sitting still at my desk for the first time of the day I realized it was 6:30pm, and I had left my phone on the desk most of the day and wouldn't you know it there were three missed calls from Rafik and a voicemail. I called in to the voicemail and there was that Barry White tone declaring, "Hey homie, you must still be working and shit, hit me up when you get this." I laughed and thought, 'Geez, this is like some school stuff, and now I'm sure he's a switch hitter; who calls that much that isn't interested. That's cute, I guess.' I intended to call him from the car on the way home but as I got in the car my phone rang out with a call from my brother Ted in Virginia. I answered to his wiped out voice, "Eddie Jimmy what's going on?"

He has called me that since we were kids; he would always tease me about having two first names. It was so hilarious, that I didn't realize until I was 10 years old that he had two first names too. I said, "What's the matter Teddy Jimmy?" He said, "Don't fuckin' play, I'm still tired from helping you pack all that bullshit. My arms are hurting and my legs are sore, but I'm on my way to the gym." I said, "Such dedication, it's a shame you have the same amount of dedication to an ice cream smoothie." He said, "Ha-ha very funny. You have your vices too." I felt like that was a great segue, so I went right in and explained that mornings strange meeting with Rafik. My brother was undeniably straight, but we were very close and there weren't many things that we didn't discuss. In his normal fashion Ted quietly listened then took a second to assess the information and came up with, "Don't make me have to come up there and bust Fiki's ass. That nigga sounds like trouble! If you want my advice, and I know you didn't ask, I would smash the nebby slut on the first floor and then see if they

20

wanted to do a threesome." I laughed loud and said, "How the hell did you come up with that?" He said, "Huh," with his I don't know why you ain't following what I'm saying voice, "What's to know, they both want some dick!" I said, "You're dumb Ted; I'm sure she don't know that nigga is on some ole, down-low shit." Ted replied, "She didn't waste anytime to make sure that the nigga wasn't before she gave him some skins. And what, were you putting on a hard act, when she was up in your face?" I said, "You know I don't do all that, I'm me 24 hours a day, she just fell for the good looks - you know the ones that ma and dad didn't give you!" With a chuckle he said, "I ain't no ugly nigga, but they knew what they was doin'. They gave me some alright looks and an anaconda, cause they knew I was goin' be drillin' holes in these hoes." I said, "Whoa there Tonto, I ain't lackin' or slackin'. I've given out a few cases of strep-throat and I've been up the broke-they-back mountain a time or two." We both exploded into laughter. After about three minutes of cracking up, my brother said,

"Okay lil' dude, all jokes aside, I'm just sayin' be careful wit' dat nigga Fiki, I don't trust his ass and I don't wanna have to come down to the Burgh and lay hands on him." I snickered and said, "Oh so now you're a preacher?" He replied, "Absolutely, they call me the honorable Reverend Pain! And I have a calling in the area of ass-woopin for the Laud." I bust out into laughter and told my brother, "I will talk to you soon, crazy ass!"

I pulled up in the front of my apartment complex and exited my car, it was a beautiful Fall evening, I was surprised there was no one on the street, it was very quiet, actually almost perfect. Coming from Baltimore I wasn't used to that kind of non-activity, it was a bit refreshing. I stood on the front steps for a moment and just took it all in. Afterwards I climbed the steps to my second floor residence, entered and looked around at all the boxes everywhere and took a seat on the couch. I thought about all the work to be done and decided in that instance, that all this would not be completed until the weekend. I

decided to make a poor man's supper, I was
too tired to get into anything else that was
going to involve extensive cooking. I put a
pot of water on the stove to boil as I heard
my doorbell ring. I walked over to the
intercom system by the door and pressed for
a visual and wouldn't you know it was my
newfound friend, Mr. Jerry. I hit the
buzzer to allow him entry to the building,
within a few seconds he was at the door
knocking a sensible knock. I opened the
door and immediately turned and walked away
to avoid staring at him; I said, "Hey Rafik,
wassup. I'm sorry about the missed calls
today, the day was crazy and when I jumped
in my car my brother called…" he cut me
short, "That's okay Playboy. I told you it
don't take me long to get over here and I
was going to a spot on this side and just
thought I'd drop in on a nigga, I hope it's
aight." I replied, "Cool, I'm just making a
poor man's supper, would you like some?" He
chuckled and said, "Sure, what's in it?" I
said, "Trust me, it's good Rafik." He
looked at me with a glassy kind of look in
his eye and said, "It's funny but I like the

way you say my name, you got an accent." I said, "Nah, you're the one with the accent Pittsburgh boy," as I turned my back and tended to my pot of water that was now at a steady boil. He came up really close behind me and stood still like a statue. I immediately froze as I felt his breath on my neck. He towered over me with his more than six foot frame. He leaned down and whispered, "Nah, it's you wit' the accent and the soft ass hands my dude." I placed the pot on an unoccupied eye and turned around, and as I rotated Rafik remained in his descended position, which caused our lips to touch briefly. My stomach filled with butterflies immediately as I felt the supple smoothness and moisture of his full perfectly sculpted kissers, I quickly covered my mouth with my hand and said, "I'm sorry, excuse me!" He stood straight at attention and said, "Fo' real though," he paused, then continued, "Ed J. - I'm not." I just stood speechless as he continued, "Now I know them lips are as soft as them hands." We both stood staring each other down without a word being spoken for what seemed an eternity, though it was only a few moments. Then I heard my brother's words ringing in my head, "DON'T MAKE ME HAVE TO FUCK FIKI UP!!!!!" It snapped me from the trance, I said, "Cool man, have a seat and let me finish this." He looked at me puzzled and after a second or two he took a seat on one of the stools that sat up at the breakfast nook that rested in the beginning of my kitchen area. I caught the vibe right away that he really was puzzled at my response to his advance, there was ackward silence for the rest of the time that it took me to finish the food, he just sat with his back to me, facing into the livingroom playing with his phone. I played right past his sudden withdraw and presented him with his plate of food as I took the stool right next to him and began eating. He looked at the plate and then began to eat, after a few forkfuls of the dish he blurted out, "Ed J. what did you call this again?" I laughed; thank goodness the silence was broken; then I replied, "A poor man's supper!" He laughed out loud and said, "Fo' real dog; what's all in here my dude?" I replied,

"Chicken flavored, Oodles of Noodles with Land-o-Lakes American Cheese and pepper." He said, "That's it, this shit is so good, like dinner or some shit and all it is, is a pack of Oodles of Noodles. I can't believe it!" He kept shaking his head as he quickly cleared the plate, looking like a perfectly sculpted, 10 cent meal eating piece of artwork - I wouldn't tell a lie, the boy is so damn sexy it was just sickening.

As I began to clean up the dishes Rafik asked, "So, do you wanna hit it to the spot with me?" I replied, "Can I take a raincheck, I got so much to do and I'm already as tired as hell." He gave me this sad puppy dog eye look and said, "I'ma let you pass this time, but I'm used to getting my way, you will learn that." I laughed and said, "Wow, your deep." He stood up from his stool and walked toward me, I immediately started getting nervous. He leaned down and bit my earlobe so gently and whispered, "I like to go deep too." I backed up and said, "And your very forward," he snickered a devilish laugh and said, "I am." He then grabbed me in a full on

embrace and deep kiss and said, "How bout I
stop back by here around 2 – 2:30 and give
you a proper welcome to the Burgh?" I was
speechless as he walked out the door and
blew me a kiss from those big beautiful
chocolate lips. I swear I stood there
motionless for 10 minutes after the door
closed.

Chapter Two

"Welcome To Mt. Bentley"

For the next few weeks there was a very
heated situation building between myself and
Mr. Rafik Jerry, with an interesting and
ever-so-present involvement of the unknowing
first floor tenant, Miranda. No matter how
much I told myself, this is life and it just
is what it is. I knew it was dead wrong!
And the wrong was resting on my head because
I knew for a fact that Rafik was screwing
around with Miranda first. And to make
matters worse, she was trying her best to
become friends with me, but I kept her at an
arms length. The guilt would surely be too
much if we were actually hanging out like

good girlfriends. I had declined trips to the mall, a concert and several invites to grab a bite to eat. I was running out of excuses, but not feelings for Rafik. As much as I wanted to care less about his existence, it was just impossible. Each night that he came by I tell myself, "This is it, no feelings, just sex and nothing more," then two seconds in those lips would set my soul afire. He was so good at everything that it always became an emotionally crippling experience; from the moment of nakedness all answers became yes, hell yes and are you kidding, YES!!!!!

The worse feeling of all that is attached to the situation comes when I leave the house in the morning and see the moving truck parked out front, immediately I know that Rafik has spent the night with Miranda. Even though I've accepted these ridiculous terms, it doesn't make the pill any easier to swallow. Envy and jealousy still gets the chance to kick me in the ass, while meanwhile Mr. Jerry is having his cake and eating it too, literally. He is a very sly man that has his operation running very smoothly, but all good things come to an end. I always say, 'What happens when Miranda sees you coming from up here?' And he always says, 'That's not an issue; I will take care of it and she won't catch on. When I come see you I always drive different cars. And besides she don't even know that you fuck around, she thinks you are cute and shit.' I always just tell him, 'Whatever, I just don't want any mess, I can't stand all that.' He promises that he's never gonna get caught, and I just think to myself, 'Good luck with that!'

I'd been in Pittsburgh maybe a month and a half when one Saturday Miranda invited me to join her at her church the next day, and I obliged. We agreed to meet in front of the complex at 9:30 am the next morning. Miranda threw in a little dig, by saying, "I couldn't use the Devil to get to hang out with you; I figured I'd try baby Jesus and see if you would respond to him and let me get atcha'" I said, "Be nice, I have just been very busy with settling into work and unpacking this apartment. But we can definitely take in some good ole church tomorrow. She said, "Yes indeed, I can't wait to see your fine ass all cleaned up and ready tomorrow." She flashed her perfectly lined eyelashes and sauntered off, I laughed and thought to myself, 'She is a piece of work, but just as cute as she can be.'

I got up extra early and made myself a good breakfast and got dressed in my favorite suit, it's a midnight blue Armani suit with a fit that only a master tailor could achieve. I matched it up with a midnight silk shirt and tie, and of course Stacy Adams on foot in midnight blue for a completely perfect look. I felt good, and I was ready to go and get what word the Lord had for me on this day. I was out front and ready to go at exactly 9:30 a.m. with my midnight blue Versace shades in place. I was standing out there by myself for a short time and then out of the door came a vision of chocolate bliss. As I scanned Miranda from her foot up, the sun seemed to glisten on each piece of her as I took her in. Beautifully manicured toes that rested so delicately into a sickening sandal with the highest, spikiest heel that I believe she

could find. Soft brown knees that were
absolutely free of scars sat perfectly on
top of a perfectly shaped calf. Multicolored silk grazed each magnificent curve
of womanhood that she possessed, with her
above the knee caftan. Not one strand of
hair was out of place and all the makeup was
applied flawlessly, it was hard to believe
that it was so early in the morning; what
time did she get up and start getting
dressed?

Miranda walked up to me and rubbed the
lapel on my suit jacket so softly and said,
"I'm about ready to take you back in the
building and let you go up under my bible-
belt, shit." I just smiled and gave her a
wink. She continued checking me out and
walking toward her car, as she blurted out,
"I'll drive, and you ride with me, cause
Lord knows if you drive and I ride with you,
I'm gonna have to reapply my lipstick." I
burst into laughter as we entered the car
and said, "Cut it out Miranda, you are a
mess!" We sped off while the sweet sounds
of the tabernacle filled the vehicle,
Miranda sang along and was quite good.

Before long we pulled up to one of the hugest, most gorgeous churches I have ever seen. I got out of the car and just took in the structure and the authenticity of it's stained glass windows; it really was a breathtaking building. Miranda seemed to know everyone, she sauntered through making her presence known, hugging the necks and pecking the cheeks of mostly the male members of the congregation. It didn't take long to notice the distain of some of the counterparts of those receiving her attention. Eye cuts and rolls were prevalent as we strolled close to the front for seats. As I sat down I continued to take in the sights, crisp new bibles on each pew, soft organ music being played, white gloves, big hats and tons of soft chitter-chatter. Very reminiscent of my home church in Maryland. As the service began the choir was undeniably talented, their voices filled that huge church almost effortlessly.

As the selection drew to a close a beautiful white robe adorned in slight bits of purple and metallic gold floated into the pulpit, at the bottom was the most beautiful

pair of heels in gold with straps delicately
wrapped at her ankles. At the top of the
robe was way too much hair, we were about a
half of a bag of weave from a Diana Ross
80's look. The mound of hair hung literally
mid way down her back, and as she slowly
turned around to face the onlooking over
anxious crowd, she revealed a RuPaul's Drag
Race face of makeup. I said, "Miranda,
who's that?" She chuckle and said, "Oh
geez, that is Pastor Pearline DiPuu. She is
the associate minister and the praise and
worship leader. Just watch her, she always
gets everyone into the spirit of praising."
I smiled a brief smile and did as I was
told, thinking to myself, "Let the clown-
mania begin!" I could just tell that
something here was going to force me to hold
my laughter in.

I watched in awe as Pastor DiPuu
swirled into the pulpit and grabbed the
microphone and broke into song, very loudly
I might add,

Welcome, into this place

Welcome into the broken vessel, thank you Jesus

And just like that, she broke out of the song and started speaking in tongues and carrying on, "When I think about the goodness of the Lord, Ohhhhhhh!" She began shaking her hair from side to side wildly and yelling, "Thank you lord, thank you Jesus!!!!!" And then came the running back and forth in the pulpit from one side to the other. As she performed her obvious, foolishness ritual, the congregation bought in and began hollering out in acceptance of her ridiculous behavior. It just geared her up to move forward with the show. She took a spot in the center of the pulpit and slammed her hands on her hips and yelled, "I feel it! I feel it! I feel my help coming – Yes, yes, yes, yes, yes – My help is here!!!!!" She jumped up and down in place and started to shout and dance at an almost impossible rate of speed. Miranda looked over at me, snickered and said, "Told ya, she is a fool. But she gets this church rockin'." I had only taken my eyes off of

Pastor DiPuu for a split second but when I looked back at her she was proceeding out of the pulpit in a full on sprint. She ran down the center aisle of the sanctuary at top speed while screaming, "Yes Lord! Yes Lord!!!!!" She ran back down the right aisle, across the front, up the left and then returned back down the center aisle and as she approached the steps to the pulpit, she just collapsed onto the steps on all fours. She rolled over on her back and laid completely out and yelled out, "Yes God, you are good, yes Savior, you are so good!!!!!"

I was so sure that this went on every Sunday, the biggest reason I believed this is; when she collapsed, not one usher moved to assist her. They have to be used to this going on. She laid on those steps for what had to be ten minutes getting herself together and instructing the congregation to offer the Lord and hand clap praise. The members began clapping and chanting, "Yes Lord!"

After a few moments Pastor DiPuu had caught her breath and returned to her feet, she took her place behind the podium on the left side of the pulpit. She raised her hands high and started, "Next to the pulpit, I would like to bring a man, a mighty - mighty man of God! He is ours, sent to us with a blessing from the most high! Ladies and gentlemen I give you Mt. Bentley's very own - Pastor Kareem Bentley!!!!!"

In that instant the lights went as bright as they could, the choir stood to their feet as well as the rest of the congregation. The musicians went into overdrive and all the focus was on the back of the church. On the left side a door opened and out walked a brown-skinned male that stood about 6 foot 1 inch tall with a bald head, and very sturdy frame. In unison on the right side a door opened and out walked a light-skinned, sturdy framed specimen about 5 foot 11 inch tall, with curly hair and the same cocky walk as the bald guy. They both walked toward each other and met at the center aisle and stopped. You could feel the anticipation building in the sanctuary as the door on the right side reopened and out walked a black robe filled out to perfection with the frame of an Adonis with a head of perfectly, freshly twisted dreadlocks pulled neatly into a ponytail. The statuesque figure moved to the center aisle and began forward to the pulpit, while his new world disciples or henchmen, as I like to call them, followed by his sides, but ever so slightly behind him. It was like a scene from a movie, and this dude was seriously in a mode that he is the Gladiator or the God of this temple. As he made his entrance, all of the onlookers stood and clapped as if this were some ritual. I just looked on in awe, I couldn't believe what I was witnessing, it was very cult like. As he passed our pew, I couldn't help but notice that Pastor Kareem Bentley was undeniably one of the most gorgeous men that I had ever laid my eyes on, and yet he looked so familiar to me, I could've sworn that I've seen him somewhere before. But I just figured maybe I caught him on a magazine article or some kind of advertisement or something, or maybe it was just a fluke, but what was real is that the reverend was fine.

Miranda whispered to me, "All the hoes in here want a piece of that, but it's not gonna happen, his wife has that thing on lock." I smiled and whispered back, "Clink, clink." We chuckled and continued to pay attention to the service and it's odd way of conduct. I had never been to a church like this, and had never seen or heard of some of the practices that were taking place. At one point they were asking for offerings in specific denominations. I personally felt like that was a bit much, but I was just visiting. The offering segment of the service was so long that I felt like I was at a visit on Wall Street or at some undercover auction for salvation. I just shook my head and thought, 'Boy, I can't wait to explain this church service to my mom. I'm sure she would be able to explain some of the things that were odd to me, and if she can't, hell, we will have a good laugh.'

I did notice that when Pastor Kareem dealt with the congregation, he more or less flirted with them to get what he wanted done. He would shoot them looks to melt

them and it seemed as though they were all
under some kind of spell. Even down to the
choir director, who was obviously a little
light in his loafers. He shot ole boy a
look and he knew to come sashaying with a
bottle of water. I was really tickled with
it, I said to Miranda, "Damn, is that
songstress chasing your pastor too?" She
laughed and said, "There is someone from
every corner that is working to get that
dick. But that sissy will never get it,
he's so dumb." I just said, "Okay." I felt
it was time to let that go. As the service
grew to a close, I was really ready to go,
but Miranda wouldn't leave until she
introduced me to Pastor Kareem. As we
approached him, I could tell that he was a
little under the Miranda spell, as was she
under his. She grabbed my hand and said
sweetly, "Good afternoon Pastor, the service
was as lovely as ever. I couldn't hardly
sit still." The pastor's right eyebrow
raised just a little and he had a slight
lustful look in his eye as he responded to
my slick but slutty friend, "I'm glad you
enjoyed my,(eh-hum, he cleared his throat)

the spirit getting up underneath you sister, it's always good to see your beautiful face on a Sunday morning." She smiled and said, "Likewise; this is my friend Edwin James, he is new here from Maryland, he is a writer." He extended his hand and took a firm grip on mine and I immediately felt the magic of Pastor Kareem working on me, his voice shot through me like fire as he said, "A writer huh, well it's really nice to meet you, maybe you will choose us to be your church home while you are here, that would be really nice." I said, "We'll see, I thank you for the invitation, I did have a wonderful time this morning. By the way, do you ever come to Maryland, Virginia or DC area, you look so familiar." He said, "Not for a lot of years now, I used to get down there for a lot of gospel conferences and I also spent one year at Howard. No telling we may have crossed paths before, God's people tend to do that, especially before he puts them together to do his work, so you should really consider us at Mt. Bentley, you already have one good sign." Then he did it, he flashed a beautiful white smile,

I about melted. I said, "I will definitely
give it some thought, thank you Pastor." We
stepped out of the way, there was an obvious
line forming behind us. As Miranda and I
made our way to the door we were stopped by
a voice that rang out, "Miriam, Miriam
Dear!" Miranda grabbed my arm, clenched her
teeth and said, "Damn," as she stopped and
turned, it was Pastor Pearline DiPuu. She
rolled right up and said, "How rude Miriam,
you weren't even going to introduce this
fine young man to me. Were you planning on
keeping him all to yourself as well." She
followed the sly comment with an ever so
shady chuckle. By this time Pastor DiPuu
was out of her robe and she really wasn't a
bad looking woman, her body was in good
condition for her age; she had to be in her
mid-forties, just entering cougar-stage.
Yet still too much hair, nails and makeup.
Miranda responded to her by sighing so
sweetly with a half baked grin, "Listen
DiPuu, I've told you before, my name is not
Miriam and Edwin introduced himself to you
right along when he stood with the rest of
the visitors, there is no reason that you

41

needed a personal introduction; not that I can see." I said to myself, 'Uh-oh you can smell the catnip in the air.' The pastor threw her mound of hair back as if at a Ross concert and stated, "I am the associate minister of Mt. Bentley, and that does require a significant amount of respect, Melanie. I'm sure if you have parents, you've been taught better than that." Miranda's eyebrows shot so high up on her forehead I was tempted to try and catch them. She leaned all her weight to one side in the sexiest ghetto girl stance you've ever seen and said, "Let me tell you something, this is the last time we are going to have one of these little petty conversations. I don't bother anyone when I come here but for some reason this is the third or fourth time that you feel the need to push your foolishness my way, I don't know what it's about, but I'm telling you, I don't like it." The more I listened to Miranda you could hear a New Orleans accent spewing from her lips, the madder she got. She continued, "And for the record my name is Miranda – not Melanie and not Miriam.

And as far as parents and teachings, I learned everything I needed to know, I'm not so sure who told you that this was a gymnasium and not a sanctuary. I'm just waiting on the weekend that you show you true self and come swinging in on one of these chandeliers; ya lil' sanctified monkey!" Pastor DiPuu got off into a little huff and said, "If you didn't always show up with different men you too could take in the goodness of the Lord and not have people leave you with the juice of the demon between your legs, you hellish little vixen." I interceded, "Ladies, ladies – it's okay. Pastor DiPuu, it has been a pleasure meeting you this morning, and you look beautiful. Miranda can we go?" Pastor DiPuu grabbed my arm hard like a witch doctor and said in a cryptic voice, "The Lord said, 'Watch them around you with wings, they don't all have feathers. And a bare winged harlot will fly you straight to hell.' Watch yourself my brother – she's headed downward – for everything and every reason!" Miranda said, "You crazy floor rolling, aisle running Bitch, you are

forever quoting something that ain't in the
Bible, I don't know who you think you are.
Sitting around mad at me cause you can't get
a man, try disconnecting from your crazy for
awhile and maybe someone will want you!" As
we walked away the pastor said in the same
cryptic tone, "Have a great day Harlot
Demon! And may God cover you my brother."

When we got outside the church I just
followed Miranda in silence, she was walking
top speed to her car, when we got there I
stopped her and held her in an embrace. She
reluctantly obliged, I whispered, "Don't
worry Miranda, only a few people heard what
was going on, and who even cares. She had
no right to do that to you." I could feel
that she was calming down, I let her go and
opened the door for her and then let myself
in the passenger side. She just sat there
for a moment and then said, "This is just
why I don't come every week, cause I would
be done smacked one of these clowns, or
called my gram back home and have her to
work a root on one of them so deep that they
wont be able to pull up their own stockings"
I said, "Yeah, what's that about I could

hear your accent so clear once you got
upset. Why do you cover up your accent and
how can you do it so well?" She responded,
"People here are so closed minded, that I
don't feel like explaining it or dealing
with people's preconceived notions of who or
how I am. But yes baby, I am a girl
straight from the Bayou!"

I responded, "I love the accent, it's
sexy as hell!" She said, "Thank you, and I
apologize, but I do have a real temper. But
besides all that, how did you like Mt.
Bentley Christian Church?" I said, "It was
very interesting and full of sights to see,
but all jokes aside, I would definitely
attend again."   She said, "Good, well
Welcome to Mt Bentley!

Chapter Three

"Oh Lord, It's A Fire"

"I could stay in here all night long, you got some of the best stuff in town!" I came out of the pleasure trance that I was in with that comment. I said, "Really, and

just how many of the town holes have you
drilled to make that assumption dude." My
overconfident guest said, "Hush up and lift
your legs for me and get your spine ready
for this work I'm about to give you!" I
really didn't care for the comment but I had
to keep face and act as though nothing
really mattered, I knew better than to start
this but now it's too late. I just did as I
was told and held on to the scattered
moments of lovemaking.

To my surprise Rafik decided to stay
over on this night, it didn't happen often
but when he did it just made things worse.
It was so easy to get used to being in his
grasp as you slept, he just had a gift for
lovemaking and making you feel safe, even if
it was just for a limited time. Around 4:30
a.m. as I laid in the embrace of my part-
time lover watching television and fading in
and out of sleep with the interruption of
his snoring in my ear, I thought I was
dreaming but I was very much awake. There
was a news flash about a local church
catching fire, I slid away from his arms and
grabbed the remote to turn up the sound and

I was in shock. I crawled down to the far
end of my king-sized bed, lying on my
stomach naked watching the news coverage
like a child watching cartoons. I couldn't
believe what I was seeing, it was Mt.
Bentley, engulfed in flames and firemen
fighting like crazy to get it out. After
about fifteen minutes I woke Rafik up to
make him look at it; with one eye open he
said, "Alright Boo, I see it - the shit
burned down." Then he rolled over, I said,
"That is so rude Ra; I was just in that
building two weeks ago, it's crazy to look
at it burning like that." He turned back to
me and said, "You can be such a girl
sometimes, girls think like that." I said,
"Whatever, but you know I ain't no girl
nigga." He laughed and said, "But you
holler like one, want me to make you!" I
said, "Go to hell, Rafik Jerry!" He
chuckled and said, "Only if the way there is
up in you." I replied, "You think you and
your little comments are so cute." He said,
"Oh now I'm not cute? For real, Ed J. -
Come getcha some of all this." He yanked
all the blankets off to expose his perfectly

naked frame. I laughed at him and said, "Just as stupid as hell." I got up off of the bed and headed toward the bathroom, I heard his heavy size 13 feet hit the ground as he persued me, within minutes I felt his teeth tugging at my skin and his hands tugging at everything else, this was the beginning of a heated session that last until 7:15 a.m. when he left out of the building through the back entrance to his car.

I took a shower and laid back down and was completely out until 10:30 a.m. when Miranda called and said, "Did you hear the news; Chile, Mt. Bentley is no more, it caught fire last night. Put on some clothes, let's go down and see what's going on." I said, "Okay!" I don't know who was more ready to go, the reporter in me or the nebby-queen. Either way, I grabbed my camera and we were out.

We rode together in Miranda's car, she was flying to the scene and I was belted in my seat and zooming down the road right beside her. When we got there it was a sight that took my breath away, to have stood inside of this huge spectacular church just two and a half weeks before and now it has been reduced to a pile of burnt sticks and rubble is absolutely so hard to fathom. I decided at that moment as I was snapping pictures that I wanted to do an article on the history of this great church. I told Miranda on the way back home what I planned to do, she told me she thought Pastor Kareem would love the idea. It was all set, I would approach the pastor on Sunday after the service, Mt. Bentley had such a presence in Pittsburgh that the Hill House Association offered to allow Pastor Kareem to hold his services in their auditorium, which was large enough to accommodate his congregation, until he could find another church to get in to.

On Sunday I was anxious to talk to Pastor Kareem, I was praying that he would be open to my offer to do the article on Mt. Bentley, I was so sure on the impact that article would have at the magazine I worked for, this would definitely be something that would turn the spotlight on me at the office. The service just couldn't get over

soon enough, I walked straight up to him as
he came down from the stage, his two deacons
strolled up on me just like there was some
kind of threat, I chuckled inside. I
cleared my throat and said, "Good morning
Pastor, I am really sorry about the
unfortunate happenings that have gone on,
though I am impressed as to how the
congregation is pulling together to stay
together, it is very inspiring to watch."
He replied, "Thanks, but if you feel that
way, why haven't you joined?" I responded,
"Well, I told you briefly, I still have a
home church in Maryland and that is a large
step to actually take up membership at a new
church and I just haven't been able to take
that step just yet." I watched as his right
eyebrow raised slightly, you could tell that
he was used to getting what he wants. A
slightly awkward moment of silence passed
and then he stated, "You have a point, and I
definitely don't want to push you into any
decision, even if it is the best decision."
I cracked a half of a smile and replied, "I
see." He said, "Good, was there something
pressing that you wanted to talk with me

about this morning, not being rude, but I am
running on a tight schedule today." I said,
"Indeed, what I want to ask was your
permission; I write for a local magazine and
I would love to chronicle this great church
and pay homage to it's existence. It would
entail me just getting hold to some older
pictures of the church and being able to
interview a few members of the church. I
will stay completely out of the way and keep
it very low key, but I feel the article will
warm the hearts of those who know the church
and raise the awareness of this great
entity, and we can even add information
about donations toward the rebuilding of
God's house." I watched as all of his
previous worthless chatter faded into the
background, as soon as he got to the,
'What's in it for me!' his ears were wide
open. I found it quite tacky. As I watched
Pastor Kareem eyes dance with delight and
dollar signs and thoughts of donation
envelopes, he responded, "That' sounds like
a great idea, I love the way you think – you
will most definitely be one of my flock. I
am totally in agreement with this project,

anything that shines a positive light on Mt.
Bentley, I am happy to participate in." I
thought to myself, 'What an opportunist!'
But whatever, it's time to further my career
and do what it is that I do best; write!!!!!

Chapter Four
"Thug Pastor"

Miranda and I left the Hill House and
decided to go over to the Northside of town
to have lunch at a restaurant that belonged
to a friend of hers. I was already
brainstorming on how to get to as many of
Mt. Bentley's members as possible, quickly.

We decided that current members would
be easy, all I had to do is put out an
announcement at church. And social media
would probably be the best way to find
previous members. Word of mouth should
absolutely fill in the blanks. I didn't
think I'd have a lot of problems gathering
enough information for the article.

Miranda pulled up to a section and parked the car as she explained, "Do you see the McDonald's and the 7Eleven down there on the corner?" I said, "Indeed." She continued, "If you take the left down there, that's where the two stadiums and the Rivers Casino is. When we finish lunch we can go by and I'll show you." I said, "Okay Luv, that's sounds good." I didn't have the heart to tell her that I had been to the casino several times; Rafik had taken me, it was a good time, but all times with Ra, were good times - unfortunately Miranda knew first hand how it was spending time with him.

As we approached the building, I said, "Oh my goodness, I wouldn't have even seen this place." She said, "Really, there's a big sign out front." I said, "What!" I ran back out front and there it was as big as day, 'Welcome to Carmi's.' I ran back in and said, "Miranda I don't know how in the world I missed that big sign." She laughed and said, "You are so doggone excited about that article, that's all you're focused on, but wait til you get some of this food that

my girlfriend prepares up in here." She
started clowning and rubbing her belly,
which made me laugh really hard. We
approached the front of this dimly lit,
exquisite restaurant that had an atmosphere
that makes you want to stay forever. And
not to mention all the aromas coming from
the back, I was immediately starving.
Within moments an older woman and younger
guy appeared with huge grins on their faces.
They spoke almost in unison, "Welcome to
Carmi's," the woman took her spot at the
register as she answered the phone that had
begun to ring. The gentlemen said, "May I
seat you?" Miranda turned right on like a
Chatty Kathy doll, "Sure, if you must, you
can sit me wherever you want." And followed
through with an obvious seductive glare. He
responded, "Mmmmm," and licked his lips. I
chuckled and said to myself, 'Oh my!' He
led us to a booth and sat us down. In back
of us was a table filled with older
caucasion women having lunch, and from the
volume at the table you could tell they were
having an extremely good time. The young
gentlemen said, "We will have someone over

in just a second to take your order."
Miranda responded, "Is the owner in?" He
said, "Why yes ma'am." She said, "I'd like
her to take my order." He said, "No
problem, let me see if she is available."
Miranda said, "Hold on Luv, you mean to tell
me that you would take an order to have the
owner take a customer's food order at their
request?" He responded, "Absolutely, we are
trained to give a customer the desire of the
heart if possible while dining at Carmi's."
Miranda said, "Cool, go and get her then."
I was thinking to myself, 'And you're being
a bitch to him, because...' So when he walked
away I said, "Why are you giving him a hard
time M?" She said, "Oh boy, watch how I
work this." A few seconds later the guy
returned and directly behind him was a
chocolate skinned goddess, she stood almost
six-foot and as curvy as could be. She
opened her mouth to say, "Hello, I am the
owner, and how can I be of assistance?" Her
voice was a soft, mellow and soothing as
brand new sheets on a queen size bed. She
glanced over and said, "Miranda...Girl how you
doin!" Miranda jumped up and the two

embraced, I could tell right away that they were friends from some time ago. Miranda sat back down and said, "I finally made it over here, and I'm ashamed, I should've been here ages ago. But girl, I'm impressed, this place is really sharp, and it's so, you!" She went on to say, "This is my friend Edwin," I stood up and offered and handshake and said, "Good afternoon, it's nice to meet you; I love the restaurant and it's atmosphere." Miranda chimed in, "And I know that the food will be off the hook too!!" I took my seat as Miranda continued, "Miss Honey who is the lil' cutie that seated us?" The owner replied, "His name is Larry, he just started. He's doing really well." Miranda cooed and said, "Larry; can you call him over." She said, "Sure one second, I'll go get him." She looked and said, "Watch this." A few seconds later she returned with the guy, who now really had an alluring grin on his face. Miranda said, "Hello again, Larry, it is Larry isn't it?" He looked down at her and said very deeply, "Uh huh." Miranda arched her back and said, "Is there a Mrs. Larry somewhere around?"

He replied, "No ma'am." She continued, "Good, your boss is standing here and I want to get to know you better and I need for you…" as she glared over at the owner, she continued, "to make that happen. So that is it, talk to your boss and she will set it all up, you can go back to work now, I don't want to get you into any trouble." He nodded his head with a little laugh and said, "No problem!" The owner said, "Girl you aren't ever going to change." Miranda said, "Not if I can help it." The owner took our order and left the table with a wide grin.

As we sat there awaiting our food I could overhear the conversation at the next table and the women were speaking about Mt. Bentley and how terrible the fire was. Miranda jumped right into action, she got up and went over to the table and said, "Good afternoon, surely I wasn't snooping but I did overhear you guys mention Mt. Bentley Christian Church and I thought a few of you looked a bit familiar." The one woman on the inside left of the booth said, "Oh yes honey, we are members." She went on to

explain to them that I was going to write an
article about the church's history. They
were very excited to share some things with
us. We grabbed two chairs and pulled up to
the table and away they went, they were
having a great time reminiscing about their
church and pastor. At the table were four
caucasion women, I could confidently say
that none of them were under 65. The first
woman started, "Oh honey, how I love Mt.
Bentley, it is so alive. Nothing like my
old church - all that up and down on my
knees, I haven't enjoyed spending time on my
knees since I was in my early twenties."
Miranda and I chuckled aloud as she
continued on, "And the people are lively,
not all snooty. I really liked getting up
for church and knowing I was going to have a
good time, and the Pastor DiPuu, isn't she a
colorful soul. One never knows what's going
to come out of her mouth or what directions
she going to take off in." The woman
sitting directly across from her chimed in…
"Yeah, she is borderline bi-polar or
something. Sometimes the things she does
and says are hurtful, they are things I

would never say out loud to someone. Do you
remember the time that she was screaming
about paying tithes and said that if you
don't pay your tithes that God would punish
you by emptying your bank account and make
it so you can't pay tithes or anything else.
She said it as if she had personally spoke
to God and he told her that was what his
plan was. She is a strange lady." The next
woman chimed in as our food was showing up
to the table and actually so was theirs; so
the owner and the gentleman assisting her
moved another table to give us adequate
space as if we all came together, I gave
them kudos for the hospitality. As they sat
the food in front of it's proper owners, the
woman spoke, she had a very serious look on
her face, "Well I have been a member for
quite a long time, and I thank God everyday
for Pastor Kareem and his powerful spirit-
filled hands." She started to well up with
emotion as she continued, "My son is 37 and
still lives at home with me and my husband,
he is a good looking boy and there was no
shortage of girls stopping by the house. I
would always hear sounds that I had no

business hearing in the wee hours of the
morning. But I found it very strange when I
would hear our cute little black poodle
yelping late at night, I didn't know if he
was sneaking someone else in or was the dog
watching him doing the do with his visitors.
Well the one night I was feeling really
inquisitive, so I was going to catch him in
the act, and Oh my Jesus what I found, I
needed the King to deliver me from. I just
opened the door to the downstairs bedroom
where he stayed and there he was with the
dog on top of his penis yelping as he
maneuvered her like a sex toy of some type.
I almost fainted, I have never seen anything
like that and nor did I ever want to again."
At that moment you could hear a pin drop on
the carpet. After a moments awkward
silence, she continued on,
"I immediately called upon Pastor Kareem for
counsel, and then talked my son into coming
to church with me that Sunday for service
and to speak one on one with the pastor
after service. Well the pastor during
service said, the Lord was telling him that
someone was in need of healing amongst us

and the Lord was leading him to them, he made his way right to my son and pulled him up to the front of the church and began to lay hands on him and pray over him. He demanded and yelled out, 'Spirit of Beastiality loose this brother!!!!! Help him Lord to stop touching the small animals and help him to know that they are not for pleasuring himself but to be companions to the family and not in a sexual way.' I remember like it was yesterday, he laid his hands on his forehead and within seconds my son was stretched out in the middle of the aisle. Once he was helped up to his feet he was okay and had never touched our toy poodle again. I tell you, Pastor Kareem is just amazing! And no one has spoken of that little situation, I just love the confidentiality of the congregation." I said, "That is a very good thing, that was truly on the personal side, I thank you for sharing that with us." The fourth woman at the table took her turn and said, "I just think that Pastor Kareem is a fine piece of chocolate. Oh, I'm telling you, I wish I was 20 years younger and I'd be all over

that. Girls, I love it when he delivers his
sermon without his robe, I can tell from the
bulge in his pants that he is; no offense to
anyone, a Mandingo warrior!" Everyone at
the table burst into laughter.

We thanked the ladies for their
participation and I settled the bill for all
of our lunch, which was superb. I once
again thanked the owner of Carmi's for her
exquisite hospitality and cuisine and
assured her that I would be back and would
spread a good word.

As we got into the car and headed home
Miranda and I discussed the whole
beastiality situation. She said, "That's
some ole bullshit – that the congregation
didn't discuss that shit, I heard about it
and just didn't know who it was." I
replied, "Yeah, and to think that he passed
out and was delivered, he was probably
embarrassed as hell, and fainted. I can't
believe he did all that in front of the
whole congregation, that should've been done
in a private session, not as a floor show."
Miranda agreed, and said, "Look how we just
literally walked up on four interviews, this

ought to be very easy for you Edwin." I
said, "I hope so."

The next day around 8:30 a.m. I put out
a Facebook message asking for folks that
were interested in giving interviews, it
read...

ATTENTION:

Past & Present Members of

Mt. Bentley Christian Church

inbox me if you would like to participate
in an interview for an upcoming magazine
article chronicling the amazing history of
this great institution.

Thanks in advance!

By the time I got a break around 2 p.m.
I had several inbox messages but one stood
out amongst the rest. It was titled, "Thug
Pastor." When I opened the email, I was
shocked and alarmed at it's content; the
email read...

THUG PASTOR

You are a killer of dreams,
Dressed proper and living proper it
seems.
You wear loafers instead of timbs,
But your wrongs need to come to an
end.
Every contact with you is a business
transaction,
If there's no money involved, it's not
to your satisfaction.
Dealing and selling in the church,
No matter who may get hurt.
Performing counsel in the evenings
quite late,
Are these really sessions or just
covered up dates.
Inappropriate and ever so smug,
You are not God-like; you are nothing
more than a thug.
The role you have is as a pastor,
But this feels like slavery; would you
prefer that we call you master.

I will not indulge, there's only one
master,
And his name is God, you kind sir are
just a common **THUG PASTOR**!

I'm so glad that somebody is finally going
to expose this dude. When I said too much a
year and a half ago, I got jumped and beaten
up by Kareem's personal deacons. I put my
poem on the cars of all the members of the
church on a Sunday morning and handed one in
an envelope to the pastor's secretary. The
following Sunday when I showed up for church
I was assaulted, the police were called and
did nothing, which was just proof that what
I wrote in the poem was true. Now that a
magazine will be telling the story I hope
Pastor Kareem and his organization get what
they deserve.

Joe Monshippings - former member
(p.s. - if you really want to know some
stuff contact - James Rhodes, he is on
Facebook.)

My eyes almost bulged out of my head, I knew that there were a few things going on a Mt. Bentley, but I have never heard of such behavior within the house of the Lord. I have to say, I did find humor in the way the poem described Pastor Kareem. But he is innocent until proven guilty, I didn't start this project to crucify the pastor, it was to glorify the sanctuary, but no one so far is giving me any real information about Mt. Bentley, just dirt on it's pastor.

I saved Mr.Monshippings poem and email and immediately sent a message to James Rhodes and waited on a response.

Chapter Five

"Do You Take This Woman"

Ring! – Ring! – Ring! The annoying ringer on my cell phone filled the air in the midst of the climax of a Rafik special. I said, "I have to answer that," he snapped,

"Not right now you don't." I said, "No, seriously, it may be important." He jumped straight up from the bed like a spoiled child, "And what I'm doing isn't!" I said, "Calm down, you're overreacting." He said, "Am I, see if you feel that way when all you have is that phone." I was looking to see who the call came from when that comment stopped me in my tracks. I said, "Was that some kind of childish threat." He responded, "No, but when I give you time, you need to take full advantage of that time." I said, "And I feel the same way, and don't talk to me like that Rafik." He grabbed his clothes and started getting dressed and said, "I don't need this!" He headed for the door, I said, "Grow up, I don't know what's gotten into you, but I ain't wit it!" He slammed the door and left.

I had no time for that drama, the phone message was from James Rhodes, I had emailed him two and a half weeks before to see what he had to say about Mt. Bentley. I called him back and agreed to meet with him at my office at the magazine on Monday at 10 a.m.

I was very excited because I had no idea what to expect, but he sounds like a younger man over the phone. What could he possibly have to say that would top that poem story?

Oh well now that my attitude having non-boyfriend had stormed out I had the rest of my Saturday to clean and work. It was only 9:30 a.m. I don't have a clue what got into him, that whole thing didn't make sense, but sometimes he doesn't. I am constantly asking myself, 'Why do I do this?' I don't even see Rafik enough to have to deal with any drama. Once I started getting into my cleaning, I gave him the minimal amount of thought.

Sunday morning I decided to take my own car to church and I told Miranda I would meet her there. Well coming out of the building, I seen you know who's car in the parking lot. Needless to say, she never showed up for church, it made me a little irritated and I knew that jealousy was rearing it's ugly face. But while I was sitting there enjoying the service alone, I was really checking out Pastor Kareem and it came to me where I knew him from – and it was not from a church conference, or a church anything. As I drove home I tried to get my brother Teddy on the phone which I could not, I left him a message…

Teddy please call me, I just remembered where I remembered the pastor from, you are not gonna believe it!

As I entered the building I noticed Rafik's car was still in the same spot. As I moved past Miranda's door I could hear what just left me with an empty spot in my stomach. It sound like they were breaking her couch into two pieces, in that moment, I realized the amount of feelings that I have invested in this boy, and I wanted to know, 'How in the hell did I let myself get here!'

I literally laid around for the rest of my Sunday kind of feeling sorry for myself. When the morning came I felt so much better, I was recharged and refocused, I was totally psyched about my interview in a few hours. I grabbed a little breakfast and headed in to the office.

My secretary buzzed me at 9:59 a.m. and
when I answered, "Yes ma'am." She answered,
"Mr. James I have a Mr. James Rhodes to see
you." I replied, "Go ahead Taylor and send
him in." A few moments later, in the door
walked an absolutely adorable curly haired
fellow, with deep brown eyes, a perfect lip
line, very square shoulders and very tapered
waist, perfectly accentuated with a thin
belt at the top of his navy trousers. The
trousers were a perfect fit, they grazed his
legs ever so lightly and when he sat down
you could see how thick his thighs were,
they were like football player thighs.

He reached out and grabbed my hand for
a handshake with one of the firmest grips
that I have ever experienced, and then out
of his mouth came the sexiest voice ever,
"Hey man, how you doin? I'm glad you are
doing this, I can't wait to share my story,
I think people will see this cat for what he
really is." I said, "Well let's not waste
any time; let get started." I walked back
around to the other side of my desk and told
myself, 'Don't stare; don't stare!'

He wasted no time getting started, "As I stood at the tip of the pulpit in my rented furnace with sleeves, I could feel my body temperature rising by the second. The organ player had just about taken the whole church into a comatose state with the playing of all the traditional selections. I laughed to myself, thinking about the fact that, these folks are probably looking at me and thinking I've got wedding jitters or some form of silly nervous situation going on. Well this was so far from the truth, the facts were…I was hot as hell and my drawls were too tight! I noticed I had bought the wrong size right as I was getting dressed, and my nuts were now paying the price. I have always prided myself on being one of the leaders of what I refer to as, 'The Big Dick Crew' but trust me that day I would've been happy to be in with the 'Lil Guys' Group.'

Just as I felt as though I was going to succumb to my current agony, I noticed Pastor Kareem taking his place in the pulpit. Shortly after that the organ player began to play the wedding march, and I

watched as my future began to unfold right
before my eyes." He paused for a slight
second and then continued, "I don't wanna
sound like a punk, but all of this money and
time that, up 'til now I thought was wasted,
had started to make absolute sense. I
looked down that aisle at my woman coming
toward me in the most beautiful dress that I
think I've ever seen, she almost didn't even
look real, like a perfectly sculptured and
dressed mannequin. Her pops was holding
onto her arm with all the pride that I
believe a man could contain without
exploding from the top of his partially bald
head. When the two of them reached the end
of the aisle and he handed her off to me
like we were in the 'Olympics of Life', I
noticed one tear forming in the corner of
his right eye, and I know that he noticed
the one I had in the same place – in that
moment, he and I shared a head nod in which,
he and I joined into an agreement of
solidarity referencing the happiness of this
beautiful creature that we now shared.

It was like magic when my lady and I
joined hands and approached the altar, all

of the things that were causing my
discomfort dissipated. We were forty-five
minutes behind schedule; there was an
announcement made that the pastor was in a
last minute counsel with the bride. I was
wondering, what in the hell the problem was,
but now all that was behind us. I was
standing there with a plastered smile on my
face. As we worked through the nuptials, my
mind started to drift, that kind of stuff
never holds my attention. I was smelling a
scent that was vaguely familiar, within
seconds it started to bug me that I could
not place the smell and where it fit into my
memory. My bride happened to break eye
contact with the pastor and looked over at
me and mouthed, "What's wrong?" In that
moment I could feel myself being consumed by
a feeling of aggravation; she has told me
repeatedly that my emotions tend to show on
my face. And also that I am an extremely
jealous, distrusting male. I never deny
those accusations because they are 100%
true.

As the pastor continued with the
service, a certain amount of irritation had

entered the room as I got a handle on the familiarity of the smell which I figured out was coming from my bride. The smell was that of a male fragrance worn by Pastor Kareem. I had a memory recall of it, it is very hard not to notice it; the dude practically bathes in the stuff, and when he hugs folks after church you do tend to intake a large whiff. Well on this day it seems as though his scent must have found it's way onto my girls' gown, I was always uncomfortable with his need to hug on my woman and today was no exception, I'm sorry but I just didn't trust the dude, bible or no bible."

The irritation of this whole situation was so evident in the body language of Mr. Rhodes, as if it just happened last weekend.

He continued on, "I felt horrible that my mind was working that way, but something inside me wouldn't allow me to shake those ill feelings. As we approached the portion of the service that we would exchange our vows and our rings, Pastor Kareem came down from the pulpit and stood directly in front of us. Within seconds I became extremely

irritated; at this point I was being faced
with another familiar scent and it did not
take me long to figure out where I knew it
from or the origin of the smell at that very
moment. The smell that grabbed my attention
was called 'Botanical Gardens' and it was a
body wash used by my woman, it is
unmistakable. I know it when I smell it,
because everytime I go down on my woman it
overcomes me and drives me crazy. It makes
my shit as hard as a brick. Except for
right then, I definitely did not get a hard
on; I was getting furious. Everytime the
pastor spoke the smell would burst onto the
scene. I began to get a visual of how that
smell ended up in his mouth and it sent me
into a rage. As he was speaking the sweet
scent of my woman's vagina was filling the
space where we stood and I just literally
felt myself and my anger burning on my
insides. Seconds later I felt one single
tear drop from my eye and land on my left
cheek. In the instance, I dropped my bride-
to-be's hand and repositioned myself so that
I was facing the pastor dead-on, I then
hauled off with all of the force that I

76

could, and punched Pastor Kareem dead in his mouth."

And with that admittance, Mr. Rhodes sat back in his seat and crossed his arms with such satisfaction, that it made me chuckle a little.

He then continued, "A sharp pain shot through my knuckles but I didn't allow it to stop me. The force of the blow knocked that nigga over, which made him crash into all the pretty flower arrangements, that took so long and cost so much. I immediately jumped on top of his ass and began to choke him as he struggled to get his breath and break free from my killer grip. It's my best move, nobody could ever get out once I clamp down on that ass. I was determined not to let this dude go until his heart stopped beating. The church had a complete hush fall over the sanctuary when I first punched him and then came the chaos. There were screams and shouts asking the Lord to forgive me for what I'd done. Shortly after the confusion began it was contained; the deacons and ushers came running from all directions to try to save this punk. My

family members took the stance of battle,
they didn't know why I had cold-cocked the
pastor, but they knew that I would've had to
have had good reason to act out this way.

As we were pulled apart I realized my
tux was drenched in beautiful scarlet
streaks of blood. I was happy, that was a
better gift than any toaster that anyone
could have purchased. I was expecting to be
thrown out of the church all together, but
instead, the deacons had everyone take their
seats and had me, the bride, the pastor and
both sets of our parents meet in the
pastor's office. I was thinking to myself,
'Good, you need to know that y'all ain't
fuckin' slick! Let's get the shit out in
the open!'

It was a classic scene, both of our
mothers were a wreck, they both just kept
crying.

My mom was embarrassed and I knew
that's what her tears were all about. I had
no time to play perfect on this day. My dad
was just confused.

My brides' mother was upset and crying
about the fact that the wedding was now a

shambles and an utter waste of money; her and her husband's money. Her husband was furious and had a straight – attitude. This was their home church and this nickel-slick son of a bitch was supposedly like family to them. My bride was a ball of nerves waiting on the fallout.

As a few of the ushers scampered around Pastor Kareem with wet cloths working diligently to get the bleeding to stop that was coming from the gaping hole that I left in the front of the good reverend's mouth. My bride-to-be sat and cried heavily as both of our mothers began to try to console her. All emotions were running quite high; about fifteen minutes past and the room was coming to a somewhat calm state. My Father-in-law-to-be stood in the center of the room and said, "What in the world was that? What would possess you to do this, I want an answer young man, and it better be good!" My father chimed in, "Yes it had better be James Edward Rhodes Jr!" The pastor actually had the nerve to lean back arrogantly in his chair, as if he was totally innocent and couldn't imagine why I socked him.

I flopped down into the chair that sat directly across from the pastor's desk facing him, and I said, "Really people, do you really want an answer or would you rather squash this here and leave it as is? In that moment my bride-to-be blurts out, "What the hell, James you're crazy, you have ruined my wedding and you'd better explain!" Then the pastor slipped in his two cents, "I sure want to know what would possess you to raise your hand your hand to me young man!" I yelled, "Fo'real, y'all are off the chain; so let's get in to it!" They all leaned in like they were victims and the big bad wolf was being captured; it just pissed me off more that they were playing victim. I continued, "Well first of all, I was in love with you and you decided to treat me like a sucka. All the signs were there but I chose to ignore them, you should consider yourself lucky that I don't hit women. But you claim to be so religious so I'll let your God deal with you accordingly. And remember - karma is like you, it's a rotten Bitch!" Mouths in the room dropped, she blurted out, "What! Don't you dare!" Her mother said, "Jimmy, don't you speak to her that way; and in the church…" she placed her hand over her heart, I said, "Mrs. Jones, please, this isn't the time to fall out, save that for Sunday service. All this fake church shit has gotten on my nerves, but that brings me to you, Pastor Kareem, the leader of this ridiculousness. The reason you are sitting there with teeth missing is because – as a man, I don't allow anyone to suck my woman's pussy – but me, and nigga you violated!"

Mr. Rhodes leaned back in his chair and continued to drop the story details that undeniably still sent pain straight through to his soul.

He continued, "This punk never did deny the accusations, he just sat there quiet with a look of disbelief on his face, along with everybody else in the room." He shifted his body in his chair and moved on with his story, "Such bullshit, no one had an explanation; no one really knew what to say I guess. I got up and looked at my parents and said, 'I'm done with this fucked

up ass shit, I don't wanna talk about it
anymore, I don't wanna try to fix it, and I
don't wanna see none of these fake
muthafuckas no more.' I started toward the
door and my sneaky ass, bride-to-be
hollered, 'Please don't do this, please
don't walk out on me, you said you would
never walk out on me.' I said, 'Yeah I did,
but I didn't know you were fuckin' the
pastor…' she interrupted, 'No, it wasn't
like that, let me explain!' I replied, 'I
don't wanna hear it, I don't wanna hear a
thing from you, I'm really ready to choke
your tonsils out! I'm done with you!' And
with that, I left that church and my parents
followed
behind. I ain't goin' lie to you, it hurt
me, it hurt me bad. It's been 3 years and I
have seen my slutty ex-bride-to-be, but I
still don't talk to her, what's the point,
I'll never forgive her. And I will never
get married, I wont ever put myself in that
position again. I fucks bitches and keeps
it moving."

He looked really relieved to share his
truth and I hope it was somehow therapeutic

for him, I just felt so bad that he had to
go through that. I stood up in my seat and
extended my hand which he excepted the
handshake, I said, "I'm so sorry you had to
go through that ordeal and I am even more
glad that you thought enough to share it
with me this morning, I promise you that I
will handle this information with the utmost
care and accuracy." He replied, "I
appreciate that, you know you are a really
cool dude, I didn't expect you to be." I
said, "Why's that Mr. Rhodes?" He said,
"There's part of it, man call me James, we
are about the same age. You ain't gotta be
all professional with me, we can just talk."
I said, "That's true, but not in here, I
supervise most of those folks you see out
there when you come in, so I have to keep
the professionalism up to keep the respect
level up where it should be." He said, "Oh
shit, I didn't realize that, well now I get
it, hell we should hang out sometime, I'd
like to see you with your respect level
down." We both laughed and I handed him a
business card and wrote my cell phone number
on it, I said, "Hit me on the cell, and we

can hang out, I'm pretty new here and always looking for new things to do." He said, "Cool, I'll talk to you soon, Mr. James." We chuckled again as he left my office.

Chapter Six

"The Ex-First Lady of Mt. Bentley"

After looking at my gathered information, it really wasn't looking too good for Mt. Bentley. Did anyone have anything really uplifting to say? It seemed to be old ill feelings and warnings of non-Christian behavior, it kind of gave me the willies.

The next person that I interviewed was Pastor Kareem's ex-wife. I agreed to meet with her over Sunday brunch at the Grand Concourse in Station Square, over on Pittsburgh's Southside. I told Miranda that I would be skipping church service and when I explained why, she begged me to let her go with me, but I wouldn't. It was a beautiful place complete with chandeliers and plush classic patterned carpet throughout. It resembled an extended hotel lobby, very soothing and welcoming. I recognized the former Mrs. Bentley from pictures I found online on the church's information page. She was a very well put together woman of a 5 foot 7 inch stature; a really sharp Halle Berry inspired haircut, a delicate frame and a tiny waist. We met right at the entrance of the restaurant, we exchanged a hug – she also recognized me from my Facebook page and my literary website.

As we stood in the line to enter the exquisite brunch buffet she comfortably stated, "You are even better looking in person." I smiled and replied, "I was thinking the same thing about you." We both laughed and with that the ice had been broken. From there we spoke as if we had known each other for years and years.

I sat my recorder on the table and let the ex-Mrs. Bentley talk. She immediately touched on why her and Pastor Kareem couldn't make their marriage work. And her explanation was quite colorful. She began, "Let me say right from the start – I am no longer a First Lady and never wanted to be

one! Kareem and I hooked up in high school;
eleventh grade is when I started dating the
supposed innocent pastor's son. That was a
joke – there was nothing innocent about
Kareem. Our first date was three days after
we met, we went to a movie theatre, and ten
minutes into the movie he started rubbing my
legs and carrying on, I'll never forget it.
I had on a blue jean, mini-skirt and a
fitted t-shirt with a matching jean jacket
and white Reebok tennis shoes. We were in
the back of the theatre and I always had a
hard time telling him no. He continued his
rubbing of my legs until about halfway
through the film, it was driving me crazy.
But I maintained my lady-like composure,
until he swiftly slid his finger in my
underwear and swiped my vagina's opening, at
that point I lost it. Within the next ten
minutes, he exchanged his finger with his
tongue. For the next twenty minutes I
squirmed and tried to stay quiet, as my
moans were muffled by the screams of the
actresses being slayed and the diabolical
music playing in the movie. Kareem rolled
his tongue and worked his fingers steadily

without coming up for air. To this day I
have no idea what that movie we saw was
about; all I know is my innocence was left
there in the theatre that day. And I was
okay with it.

Kareem and I got married about a year
and a half after our high school
gradauation; we both had jobs and were
enrolled in college locally. We were doing
really well, back in those days Kareem's dad
was still living and was the current pastor,
Kareem and I were more than loyal members.
Senior Pastor Bentley was an angel, he was
very good to me and Kareem in the beginning
of our marriage, his rules were, 'If you do
the things that you need to do to secure a
good life and help out around the church you
will live the life worthy of one of God's
children.' The two of us always lived by
that and he always made our way as easy as
possible. We both graduated our college
programs free of loans, we both drove new
cars, and we lived in a very plush home –
that was a wedding gift. I can definitely
say that the building fund was used to build
a life for us – now I don't believe that is

the purpose of it, but I have no complaints, it was an absolute blessing to us. I got a Bachelors Degree in Accounting and got a position working for a large law firm downtown, while Kareem also received a BA in Business Management, but went into the ministry. He was the associate minister of Mt. Bentley until Old Man Bentley got sick and passed on. It was such drama with his three siblings and Mrs. Bentley, you see – she is not Kareem's mother, and they are only half siblings. None of them were concerned with the church as long as Old Man Bentley was living, they hardly even visited him or the church. Kareem stayed by his dad's side all the way through to his last breath. A little bit of a legal battle ensued but nothing to outlandish; my law firm stepped in and squashed it. Everything that has to do with the church was willed to Kareem and only Kareem. So the fighting didn't last very long.

My transition into being a First Lady was a strange one; I was only 28 years old, which is quite young to take on such a role. And Kareem assuming the role of the head of the church; there were some very trying days in the beginning. Just the transition from an elderly pastor to a more youthful approach was an issue at times. The older members always got upset if you updated anything; they really hate change! And Kareem is a preacher who is very progressive, he puts it right out there. Sometimes the things that come out of his mouth would even shock me. Hell, sometimes the things that came out of his mouth were just down right out-of-order. The way he delivers the word is definitely not for everybody.

My challenge came about when the power shift became evident, once it was evident that Kareem was actually at the head of Mt. Bentley it didn't take long before bodies were being thrown at him with all their openings available for entry. At first it didn't bother me and I didn't even address it, but within months it got to be really disrespectful. Some of the female members that were basically after my husband, literally stopped speaking to me. I would show up for church and they would sometimes turn their heads and pretend that they didn't see me in the parking lot. If they would walk up on us together the conversation would be, "Oh, hello pastor!!!" and then, "Umm, hi First Lady." Let me tell you, it got old very fast."

She stopped for a moment and chuckled, I cracked a smile to assure her that I was attentive and I was following her intently.

She continued, "There was one member in particular that just would not let up, she was very bold in her approach and I had really had it this one Sunday in particular. She had called at about 5 minutes to midnight the night before with some emergency that got Kareem out of the bed and over to her house."

She recrossed her legs to the other side and crossed her arms as she sat back in her chair. She had a smirk on her face reminiscent of that of a little girl on the playground when someone's lying.

She took a breath and moved on, "When my husband returned at 3:27 a.m. I just sat up in the middle of the bed and waited on the explanation that I was not going to be

receptive to, no matter what. But what I
got was arrogance and fatigue. I said,
'Seriously Kareem, did you just think you
were going to lay down and you don't need to
say something to me, it's after three in the
morning.' He yelled, 'What do you want me
to say, you know what the job is and what it
entails, so go 'head wit' all that, I ain't
tryna hear that.' I said, 'The job, oh now
you're an on-call doctor, I must've missed
that – what to do you specialize in bedside
bullshittin'?' He said, "You sound stupid,
with that ole jealous shit, if I decide to
be with someone else I will tell you to go
away, as simple as that. I wouldn't be
running around lying and sneakin', I ain't
got time for all that.' I just sat there in
silence, I could not believe what I was
hearing – the coldness of it just kind of
cut my soul, and I really don't think I ever
really recovered from that conversation that
day. I never looked at him the same after
that, I felt a complete separation between
us. But I still fought for my marriage,
that next day in church we had the normal
excited to see pastor from this woman and

the, Oh you're here too greeting for me.
During the service I noticed her get up and
go to the restroom; I followed her. When
she came out of the stall, I didn't say a
word, I just grabbed her around her neck and
slammed her into the wall and secured my
grip on her and told her, 'Let me tell you
something, you are not fooling me you lonely
bitch, but I'm telling you today - back up
off of my husband or I going to do you
dirty. You don't know me and you've
obviously got the wrong idea and picture of
who I am. You think I'm nice and quiet, but
I'm not that girl at all, there is nowhere
to slip in on my marriage. I'm all the
different women he craves all wrapped in
one, I don't need no band behind me to pick
up any background notes - Do you
understand?' She called herself struggling
to get loose from my grip, her eyes were
bulging out as if she couldn't believe that
I had yanked her. I let her go and as she
swiftly headed for the door, I said, 'Excuse
me hun, one last thing, don't think that
being nasty will work either, you seem like
the kind that would go that route, but you'd

be wasting your time, I put that dick in every hole I've got - so that wont grab his attention, I already got that covered too, thanks, but no thanks if you were planning to that route - won't work - sorry!' She stormed out of the bathroom. I followed her back to her seat and leaned over her shoulder and whispered, 'Cleanliness is right next to Godliness, now go back and wash your hands, you evil dick hungry tramp.'

Kareem got really upset with me and then I noticed that she hadn't come back to the church after several weeks, I didn't care, I was glad to see her go. After that little incident I never really trusted Kareem anymore and I did ride him about his whereabouts, people said I was crazy and that I was destroying my marriage. We slowly grew further and further apart - but I still put 150% in to try to salvage what was left of the marriage, but it just seemed as though he couldn't stand me at times.

It all came to a head this one Sunday morning about half way through the service the member I had choked returned and sat

down in the first seat next to the aisle in
the front left pew as I sat in the same
identical seat on the right. After about
thirty minutes as Kareem brought his sermon
to a close, he told the congregation that he
had some really important news that he
wanted to share. He went on to say, that he
was going to be leaving his bond of marriage
to me and that I would be receiving the
divorce decree by hand delivery in my office
the following day and that the only
Christian thing would be to just agree to
the terms and sign off, as not to make it
hard on the church or it's members. He went
on to talk about how I wouldn't allow him to
do the works that the Lord called him in to
ministry for.

I just sat there in disbelief as he
went on talking this craziness, he finally
ended by saying that he thought it was for
the best that I left the church until all of
the proceedings were completed, but once the
divorce was final I would be more than
welcome to rejoin Mt. Bentley as a member of
the congregation.

I took my emotionless body and drug it down that aisle and out of that front door and vowed never to step foot back in that church ever again. And I never did!

To make a long story short, you should know that I didn't willingly agree to many of the stipulations of that divorce settlement that cut me out of everything and left me basically where I was when he and I dated. I got a very nice settlement and basically, as long as Kareem makes money, I make money! And I get to check the books often to make sure my figures coincide with my monthly payments.

As for my pew partner, you may know her, she is the new Mrs. Kareem Bentley."

I was now sitting with my mouth hanging open in shock!

Now sitting across from me with her eyebrows raised to their highest possible spot on her forehead was the Ex Mrs. Bentley scorned and disgusted - still. And I can't say I blame her. She went on to conclude her interview, "Oh and the good pastor thought he would shine in the courtroom by making reference to the fact that I cannot

have children as his reason for his
infidelity. But it was to no avail, the
judge was a woman and did not buy in to that
foolishness at all, she actually got a
little pissed and I ended up very
comfortable at the end of my divorce. To
this day I literally do not speak to my high
school sweetheart – and I don't know if I
ever will again!"

Chapter Seven

"As The Word Cums Forth"

As I lay in my bed trying to rest I was processing the craziness of the last few weeks in my head, all the interviews are in a negative light - what am I going to do with this, I can't put this madness in my magazine. Although this information is juicy, it just doesn't work for what I needed it for originally. I decided I would go on collecting my data and I will figure out what to do with it.

As the thoughts flooded my head, I centered in on the ringing of the telephone, I thought, 'Who in the world?' It was only 8:30 a.m. I picked up and said, "Hello," a deep voice greeted me on the other end, "Eddie Jimmy wassup!" I said, "Ted, you goon - where the hell have you been, I been trying to get in touch with you for days." He said, "Chill, chill - there you go acting like a lil' sister, bring it on down slick slacks." I laughed, "You're an ass." He responded, "My ass is tired, come and let me in…" I was like, "What in the hell…" but when I looked out of the window, I could see this fool walking across the lot from his silver Mercedes. I was so excited I literally dropped the phone and ran straight for the front door and down the hall to the top of the stairs. And sure enough there he was in all of his arrogant swagger looking like my father. Once we got inside the apartment he walked around and said, "This is cool, I like this little pad boy." With sarcasm I said, "I'm so glad you approve," as I chuckled. We spent the next couple of hours with me preparing breakfast and just catching up on some things. After awhile Ted said, "So what were you trying to get to me so hard for. I said, "Man, do you remember all the stuff I said about the church and writing the article for the magazine about the church? Well it came to me a few days ago where I remembered the reverend from and I almost died, and I had no one else to tell but you." Ted said, "So spill it nigga, where'd you know the cat from?" I said, "Are you ready for this?" His eyebrow raised up as he responded, "Quit playin'" I said, "I remember him from Gay Pride Celebration in DC about two years ago!"

Ted laughed for about fifteen minutes, it was just so obnoxious. He finally said, "No wonder you can't find anything nice to say about the reverend, he isn't nice. That nigga got secrets, and secrets always come out to bite you in the ass. His ass must be feeling a lil' tender lately!" I hated to admit it but Ted was right. He continued on, "And where is that Fiki nigga at, I need to lay the fear of God in that nigga's heart before I leave tomorrow." I explained that I hadn't seen Rafik in almost a month, after his little temper tantrum. Ted said, "Good, I didn't like that nigga no way!"

The next morning I seen my brother off and Miranda and I headed off to Sunday service. On the way to the service Miranda kept going on and on about how fine my brother was. I laughed and said, "I kinda' figured you felt that way, he was down there talking to you for the longest, so he must of thought you were pretty interesting as well." She said, "I think so; he must eat a lot of pineapples." I said, "Yeah he does, but what made you bring that up? Did he ask you for some?" She said, "No, I could taste it cumming through him!" I coughed and said, "Oh duh! Miranda, you are as crazy as a road lizard." We both laughed and made our way to church in our chariot of sinful talk.

As we entered the Hill House Auditorium we were a few moments late and the service was already in full swing and the folks were up and connected - it was jumping in there like a block party. And leading the crowd like the lady with the 99cent chicken wings was Pastor Pearline DiPuu in her usual splender. She was wearing a multicolored caftan made of silk that was flowing like a river of gay flag colors with all the dramatics of the gay parade as she made her way up and down the center aisle going through her normal antics. I chuckled as we took our seat, the only thing I could think was, 'Lord have mercy, if we changed the musical selection - you would swear that we

were at a fierce drag show, Work Out
Pearline, Bitch!!!!! Somebody get her some
tips.' The thought of it kept me chuckling
for the next ten minutes - this church is
like a 3 ring circus at times.

They finally finished up with the
'Clownfest' I'm sorry I mean the 'Praise and
Worship' portion and folks finally took
their seats. Pastor Kareem got into the
pulpit and immediately went into 'The
Offering' portion and introduced something
to his congregation that I had never heard
of. He explained, "Saints, as you know,
we've been blessed to be in this
establishment rent-free until we find
ourselves another home. Well I've found us
a place! It's right around the corner,
there is a big church around the corner that
hasn't been used in a few years, everything
is in tip-top shape, the rent is a little
steep and that is why it has been empty, but
together we can make this happen. What we
are going to do is see who is really serious
about their membership to Mt. Bentley - and
how we're gonna do that is by forming two
lines down the center aisle, the line on my

right are my Mt. Bentley warriors - they
need to get in that line with $100.00 in
their hands ready to give this morning. On
the left side of me are warriors in training
- they need to get in that line with $50.00
in their hands and ready to give! This is
the only offerings that we are accepting
today, raise up saints and show me how
strong your faith is - the Lord loves a
cheerful giver!!!!! I want to see smiling
faces accompanied with 50s and 100s - I am
now turning you over to the hands of the
ushers - Bring it on down saints!!!!!" He
arrogantly turned his back and took a seat
at the center of the stage and watched as
the lines began to form. I had never seen
anything like it in all my life, it was an
absolute turn off to me. How in the hell
can you demand specific denominations of
God's people, it was just ridiculous, and
what a jackass.

When the ushers got to our aisle,
Miranda and I stood, but as we were being
led to the line, I told Miranda, "I'm
amongst those who doesn't have the proper
denomination and I'm going to the restroom,

I'll meet you back in our seat." She cut
her eye and whispered, "Edwin, you have it."
I responded, "Of course I do, and this is an
excellent training lesson for you of how to
keep it." I smiled smugly and made my way
to relieve myself. As I entered the huge
restroom it was surprisingly empty, or so I
thought; As I stood in front of the urinal
and started to take care of my business I
could hear a shuffling that was way to
familiar. A belt buckle hanging free,
muffled voices and moderate to heavy
breathing - let's just say the spirit was
moving in one of the stalls while the
service was going on upstairs for the rest
of the members of Mt. Bentley Christian
Church. This whole scene reminded me of a
Sunday night in the bathroom of the dance
club Tracks/DC back in the day - ridiculous,
I was saddened for a moment by realization
of all of the fabulously devious non-
christian-like behavior that took place in
that joint, mmmm-hmmmm, Good times!

I finished up and walked over to the
sinks to wash my hands I felt it was my
position to act just like I didn't make the

discovery that I had, what the hell, let them have their fun; there was just as much foolishness going on upstairs that was in the program. Though I have to admit, the nebby side of me really wanted to know who was just boldly getting down - As The Word Cums Forth!

Within seconds my questions were answered, I believe the water coming on startled them and out of the stall came none other than one of Pastor Kareem's right hand men. He was moving quickly and straightening his pants; he walked up to the sink washed his hands quickly and said, "God Bless you Brother," and nodded his head, I replied, "Same to you," fighting not to let my eyes roll up in my head. That was the dumbest move in the world, why not just stay in the stall until I left. I find closeted gays to always be slow, they are so consumed with not getting caught that they are constantly telling on themselves, duh! *Mr. Slick* made a mad dash for the door as I was still drying my hands, I just chuckled to myself. But before I could get going, out of the same stall came Kyle, a cute little

sixteen year old from the choir. I felt
like someone had hit me with a damn rock,
the sight of this was just sad. He thought
he was being all grown and taking control of
the situation, but he was really pathetic
and being taken advantage of by the
situation and it really bothered me, and at
this point I couldn't mind my business.
When I was still in the bathroom I could
tell that it startled him, he couldn't keep
eye contact with me, he just said, "Good
morning," and made his way to the sink and
when he looked at himself in the mirror, he
was as mortified as I was. He had two very
prominent streaks of good time juice going
down his cheek, under his chin and his shirt
was a bit stained in the collar. I could
tell that the embarrassment was almost
bringing him to tears, so I said, "Kyle, I
got you, don't worry, we all have our
secrets – this one will be yours and mine.
Let me help you clean yourself up, but you
have to promise me that you slow your roll a
little bit, you got plenty of time and he is
an ass, he could've given you a heads up or
something, you didn't deserve that. And

that's why he is preying on young dudes. Oh that shit makes me mad." He was very quiet and didn't respond at first and then he said, "Ok, thanks. And what's your name?" I said, "It's Edwin." His high-pitched voice rang out, "Okay, the girls been buzzin' bout you. All the queens in the choir said they want some." I said, "As flattering as that is; none of you are even twenty, a chill out is an order young man." The scolded poodle look returned as I told him, "Now let's get to where we are both supposed to be, and let this be just what it was - a dirty little secret - take it to the grave."

Pastor Kareem was more than half way through his message when I got back to my seat, Miranda said, "What the heck, what were you doing?" I replied, "Took a minute but everything came out great." She said, "Well that was disgusting." I just chuckled. Before long we began to line up around the front of the stage for communion, I was hoping it just went smoothly because with all these people it could possibly take forever. To my surprise it was one of the

most organized things that I had ever seen
go on at Mt. Bentley. Several ushers helped
with the handing out of the wafers and grape
juice in miniature cups. As you got your
wafer your sever would whisper, "This
represents the body of Christ." And then
your juice, they'd say, "This represents the
Blood." It was quiet, decent and
surprisingly in order. I was doubly shocked
because our server was none other than
Showgirl DiPuu. Once everyone had their
supplies the pastor began; everything
continued on smoothly until he instructed us
to break the wafer in half and eat it. The
serenity of the communion atmosphere was
broken by a slight cough that got louder
until it became a complete hacking.
Everyone lifted their heads to see who it
was; it was a familiar face to the rest of
the congregation; Pastor Melvina Wells.
This prior member who was visiting on this
day used to lead praise and worship at Mt.
Bentley until Pastor Pearline joined and the
friction between them became very evident
and Pastor Wells eventually left Mt.
Bentley. At this point everyone was pretty

much staring at Pastor Melvina who was now drinking her juice to clear her throat before instruction was given for the juice. I could see Pastor DiPuu approaching, I figured that she was going to see if the other pastor was okay and then get her more juice so that we could move on. But when she got over to where Pastor Melvina stood(who had ceased choking at this point) she just stood there and gave her a stare down. It was very curt and accusatory, as if she was trying to steal the shine or something. I just watched and in the pit of my stomach I knew something was not right. All at once, out of the quiet, Pastor Pearline yelled at the top of her lungs, "DEMON!!!!! I told you all once before she was a demon in our midst. You've choked on the bread of life because your soul is dead and black – you cannot insert the body of Christ where the Devil is residing – I rebuke you Satan – leave this place and leave us in peace you monster of the other world!!!

The room grew absolutely silent as we awaited Pastor Melvina's response. You

could see in the height that had been
reached by her eyebrows on her forehead that
she was not pleased. I had butterflies in
my stomach as I thought, 'What else can go
on in this joint today?' Before I could
finish the thought Pastor Melvina said,
"Forgive me Lord, you know my heart!" She
walked out from the group of folks to the
center spot of the stage where the remainder
of the cups of juice were sitting on a tray.
She picked up the tray and added it to
Pastor Pearline's outfit and said, "Now
you've been covered with the blood, and
trust me you will need the covering if you
don't let me alone!" Pastor Pearline took
and slapped her across the face with a sound
shattering crack; without a second's notice
Pastor Melvina began beating her on the top
of the head with the tray that the juice had
been resting on. It was the most deafening
sound; everytime she connected with the
metal tray it sound like someone was
sounding off a bell. The two of them were
finally pulled apart by Pastor Kareems
henchmen, the one had Pastor Melvina holding
her around her waist and he had taken the

tray away from her; while the other one was
assisting Pastor Pearline up from the
ground. Then we had a really scary moment,
she was mumbling something and you really
couldn't make it out, but it was the same
thing over and over. Then it started
getting louder and louder. She was saying,
"It's the power of Christ the compels you,
it's the power of Christ the compels you!"
She was screaming it in such a way, I
thought she had snapped, until she switched
over and started screaming, "You fucking
Bitch!!!!!" and started trying to make a
break for Pastor Melvina. It was a mess and
I had literally had enough, I told Miranda,
"I'm ready to get out of this place, it is
just ridiculous today." She replied, "I
know, let's go." We preceded towards the
front door and coming in the door was a huge
shock, it was like I was looking at a ghost.
Walking toward us was none other than,
Rafik. He walked right up to us and began
speaking to Miranda, "Bitch, you really are
trying me! Let's go!" I just looked, I was
totally confused. I looked at Miranda, she
said, "I'm okay Ed," I said, "Alright." I

could see Rafik roll his eyes up in his head. I walked over by the door and waited for her to finish her conversation. The next thing I know he was pretty much dragging her by her arm and she was pleading with him that she was not going with him. As they passed me and started down the front steps of the Hill House, I tried to intervene. I said, "Please, if she doesn't want to go with you, just let her go." My comment infuriated him, he didn't say a word he just turned around and punched me dead square in the mouth. I was in shock, and by the time I regained my senses I was being dragged on the cement and being kicked and punched repeatedly while Miranda begged for someone to stop him. Once I was freed from his grip, Miranda and I made a dash for her car, I was pretty sore and limping, I could not believe what was going on in this moment. How could he treat me that way, and I hadn't done anything to him, what a jerk. I climbed into the passenger seat and tried to calm down, but I was really starting to get pissed at the whole situation. Once Miranda closed her door and started the car she turned to me and said, "Thank you for standing up for me, he used to be a really nice guy but those drugs have got him trippin'." And as soon as she said it, it all made sense. The mood swings and his absence; how could I have been so blind, it completely escaped me, I didn't pick up on any of the signs. But he didn't steal from me or even ask me for anything, he just started to get very argumentative and then disappeared, I guess I was lucky. Miranda continued on to explain how he stole money from her purse and she tried to convince herself that it was not him, but it happened two more times. Then in Miranda fashion she said, "Chile I knew the nigga was gettin' high when the dick was trash. He always had some good ass dick and all of a sudden he couldn't stay hard, I knew then that I definitely had a crackhead on my hands and I was not going to indulge any further." We both laughed as we made our way home.

Chapter Eight

"And The Winner Is"

I was praying that the swelling from the after-church beating would go down quickly. I decided to work from home on Monday, but I was scheduled to do an interview over at a salon in the East side of town called Flossy's on Tuesday and I definitely did not want to be explaining bumps and bruises, how embarrassing. I spoke briefly to Miranda when she came up to check on me, she said that she hadn't heard anything from Rafik, and she wasn't interested in seeing him, she said she just wanted him to go away. I wasn't all that keen on seeing him either, I really would've like to run him over with my car. I have never dealt with anyone who put their hands on me before, it wasn't a good feeling, what nerve that took.

I woke up bright an early on Tuesday morning, all the swelling was down, the soreness and bruises had passed on and I was feeling 100%. I went in to the office and caught up on a few things before I headed over to East Liberty for my 2 p.m. meeting with Miss Bernice. I pulled up to Flossy's Hair Designs and I lucked up on a parking spot right in front. It was a cute little salon accented with a beautiful pink trim which really did go along with the theme of the name. When I thought of Flossy's, I immediately thought of a small country salon with lots of updos and spiral sets. Once I was buzzed in, I found that it was everything but that, it was a huge establishment and very up to date. I was greeted by the cutest little fly girl I had seen in Pittsburgh since Miranda. She wore

a short tapered haircut that was wrapped to
perfection, very little make-up and she had
a serious frame. She had just enough junk
in her trunk to make traffic halt. And when
she opened her mouth out came such sweet
sounds – her voice was so welcoming as she
stated, "Welcome to Flossy's, I am the
owner, how can I help you?" I replied,
"Hello my name is Edwin James, I'm supposed
to meet Miss Bernice. We were supposed to
do an interview." She said, "Great, we were
expecting you, she is really excited.
Follow me."

I followed her to the back of the
salon, once you went beyond the wall it was
huge, there were mounds of work stations and
most of them were occupied with a
hairdresser or a barber and shampoo stations
a plenty. The atmosphere was very light and
really a joy to be in. She pulled me up a
chair next to her station where the
grandmother figure, Miss Bernice was sitting
and motioned for me to have a seat, then
said, "He's here Mama Bern, and just a cute
as he can be." Then I heard this husky
voice say, "Well move your lil' butt chile

and let me get a look at the specimen." The
salon owner moved to the side and she was in
full view - the cutest, fluffiest lady I had
laid eyes on in a long time. The sight of
her made you want to just hug her, because
deep down you knew she would smell like
fresh baked cookies. I could only imagine
that she had tons of kids and grandkids.
She smiled and said, "You are a cute lil'
one aren't you, come and give me some
suga'," I laughed and went over and hugged
Miss Bernice and in the midst of it she took
a squeeze of my hind parts and said, "Yeah
girl, nice tight butt - I always liked a man
with a nice tight butt." I laughed and took
a seat - when I was really mortified, Miss
Bernice had to be in her 70's, but she was
just as alive as any 20 year old I knew.

She said, "So let's get started; now
what do you want to know about Sodom &
Gomorrah?" My eyes got wide as I tried to
hold in the laughter, the salon owner
chuckled as she continued curling Miss
Bernice's hair. She continued, "I used to
be the secretary of the church for years
dating back to when Old Man Bentley was

still living, and shortly after his passing Kareem and I just couldn't see most things eye to eye and he fired me. Now don't get me wrong, the funds for that church have never been on the up and up, but Kareem is so arrogant that misappropriation of funds is just simply an understatement." She stopped and looked at the salon owner in the mirror and told her, "You better tell him honey, you know I shoot straight from the hip, and I don't care who's feelings get hurt — if you can't handle the truth, then you need to walk a fine straight line." The owner nodded her head in agreement as Miss Bernice continued on, "I'm completely convinced that the fuels of hell and the abundance of sin is what burned that church to the ground. Along with some gasoline poured by someone who stood the chance of collecting, catch my drift? It just isn't right, the Lord is not pleased when the sanctuary becomes the devil's playground! Mt. Bentley has some of everything going on up in there, and has for quite a few years — including Kareem. You do know his origins don't you?" I said, "No ma'am, I've heard a few things about him and how he runs the church but no one has said anything about him growing up in Mt. Bentley." She said, "I bet they didn't dare tell any of that lovely story."

Her eyebrows raised up really high with a devious grin as she continued, "See when you hear folks say that Kareem is a fixture at Mt. Bentley, they really mean that. He was conceived right there in that church." A hush fell over the salon as everyone seemed to tune in as Miss Bernice dished the dirt, "He does not belong to Mrs. Bentley, Kareem is a bastard. That's why he acts that way, such entitlement – always thinking someone needs to do what he wants them to do. See, his birth mother and Old Man Bentley have always tried to repay him for the embarrassment of their indiscretion – to no avail, nothing is ever going to be enough for him. He is consumed with greed and entitlement! His birth mother is still living, she was not a nice woman and still isn't. She was in her 30's when she started up with the late Reverend Bentley, he was already in his 50's. She was an overactive member of the church, or what I would refer to as a holy-rolling whore – she had a husband and two other children. She worked side by side with our First Lady, she was almost like her right hand, they had what seemed to be a beautiful friendship. They ran several groups and programs at the church together – yet she was committing the ultimate betrayal. She screwed the pastor like clockwork, every Wednesday night after bible study. I'll never forget the day when I came back for my bible and seen her spread eagle on the pastor's desk and him banging her just like she was the First Lady, I wanted to throw up. I never said a word, I just eased out of the building – then I noticed how she always stayed after everyone else on Wednesdays. She was a lucky harlot for a long time, she swallowed that baby hundreds of times, but I guess her luck ran out, because one of those Wednesdays he managed to get Kareem up in her behind."

An outburst of laughter erupted from one of the barber's stations, but it didn't stop the dish, she continued, "She carried that baby full term and everyone thought it was her husband's baby until Kareem was born and the rumors started to swirl. Kareem's looks were undeniably similar to the three Bentley children, and the more the rumors circulated the more tension was building in the church, you could see the looks being exchanged with her husband and the pastor during service. By the time Kareem was 4 months old, the family stopped attending Mt. Bentley and then the unthinkable happened…" the whole salon was hanging on the end of it's chair at this point, as Miss Bernice continued, "We were sitting in church this one Sunday and as Old Man Bentley was delivering the message he was interrupted when a loud deep voice shouted, 'Preacher Man, you are a hypocrite and that's cool for you, because the God I serve deals with people like you! But what I am not going to do, is raise some other man's baby.' He walked right down to the pulpit and laid Kareem on the floor and said, 'Here's your bastard, you raise it, and stay away from my family or I will have to beg God's forgiveness for taking your life!' He walked out and we never seen any members of

the family again. Our First Lady picked
Kareem up off of the floor and she raised
him just like he was her own. But through
the years you knew and could see that Kareem
was undeniably Pastor Bentley's, he is just
as slick as fish grease, he can't be
trusted, he was a mess from just a little
child. But what can you say, he got it
honest, his momma and his daddy were sneaky
little liars. As the years went on it
wasn't hard to see that Pastor always
favored Kareem to his three siblings, and
the siblings noticed as well. First Lady
always managed the drama, she really was a
good woman. Each of the siblings reached
high school, graduated, left for college and
never returned – other than for visits and
that wasn't very often. Kareem stayed right
up underneath his father, and wouldn't you
know he ended up with just about everything
when Old Man Bentley passed. The last time
I remember seeing all of the siblings
together was at Pastor's funeral and before
that was at the First Lady's funeral three
years prior."

I sat up straight in my chair and let out a small sigh, Miss Bernice said, "Oh honey, there's nothing nice to be said, that place was a mess years ago and Kareem has taken it to a whole new level of blasphemy. I stayed with him as the secretary for a while but he was getting outrageous and I am too old to be keeping secrets and going to hell for someone else's indiscretions. I started to speak up and shortly after that Kareem fired me, and trust me my feelings were not hurt. Now I'm a member of a really nice church over in the Penn Hills area, you should come and visit us sometimes." I said, "You know what, you have my word, I will come to visit your church, I appreciate you doing this interview Miss Bernice and I thank you for letting me disrupt your salon this afternoon." I gave Miss Bernice a quick peck on the cheek and the salon owner walked me out.

My mind was spinning with all sorts of ideas that could be done with this information that I have gathered in the last few weeks. The one thing that I knew I couldn't do is put it in the magazine, I didn't have enough positive information to even stretch out enough to get a whole article. Then I thought, I'll give this one more try, there was a singing competition coming up in two weeks as a fundraiser and celebration of Mt. Bentley moving in to their new building. That should definitely give me enough to shine a positive light on old Mt. Bentley Christian Church and it's overly interesting pastor.

Chapter Nine

"Not In Here"

After a week and a half of quiet
Miranda and I were sharing a bottle of wine
and listening to some really good music. It
was the perfect Friday evening, we were both
excited about going to the Gospel Music
Challenge the next day at the new and
improved Mt. Bentley. There were soloists
and choirs coming from tons of surrounding

areas, I felt this would really be the turn
around for my article.

It was starting to get late when we
heard Miranda's door bell ring, she looked
on the visual screen and said, "Oh geez,
it's Rafik." I said, "Just don't let him
in." She said, "Usually I wouldn't but I am
a lil' horny after sitting here drinking
this wine." I laughed and said, "I'm out."
She said, "Okay baby, I'll see ya in the
morning." I said, "And on time – 11:30
a.m." She said, "I got it."

As I was leaving out of her door, I
passed Rafik in the hallway, I just kept
moving – he said, "Hey Yo, I'm sorry." I
rolled my eyes at him at kept going up the
steps to my apartment, I wanted absolutely
nothing to do with him. He didn't even look
the same, the toll of the drugs was showing
up, his skin was very dry looking and the
once beautiful muscle tone was disappearing,
he was appearing to become thin, it really
wasn't a good look.

Once I got up to my apartment I
realized that I was a little tipsy, I jumped
in the shower and laid myself on down. I

was in a good slumber when I was awaken by
the flashing lights and sirens out front. I
woke up completely once I stood in the
window and noticed they were in front of our
complex, I threw on a robe and slippers and
headed down the stairs. The hallway was
filled with policeman and detectives and
there was tons of people outside, but I
noticed right away Miranda's door was open
and her apartment was the focus. I said to
one of the policeman, "Where's Miranda?" He
said, "Who are you?" I replied, "My name is
Edwin James and I live upstairs, I'm really
getting worried, I'm sorry can you tell me
where my friend is?" He took me by the arm
and said come with me, as he led me outside
I got a glimpse inside of Miranda's
apartment, the furniture was thrown about
and things were broken but the most alarming
thing was the blood that was everywhere. A
tear immediately dropped from my eye as we
made our way outside I seen paramedics and
ambulances and then I seen a black body bag
on a stretcher sitting right at the back of
a coroners vehicle. I screamed out,
"Miranda, NO-NO-NO!" As I fell to my knees

almost knocking the policeman down that was
leading me. He said, "Sir, please calm
down. When is the last time you seen your
friend." I said, "Just a couple hours ago.
Where is that bastard, where is he? Did you
all get him?" The policeman said, "Who
sir?" I said, "His name is Rafik, he did
this, I know he did this!" He said, "Can
you come with us to make a statement?" I
said, "I sure will, you've got to get him,
his crackhead ass has gone to far. Oh God,
I can't believe this is happening, I told
her not to let him in!" The officer loaded
me into a squad car and I was taken to the
police station, after hours of sitting and
questioning I had divulged everything about
the fight at church and again how I told
Miranda not to let him in. The officer
shared with me that the body in the bag was
not Miranda, it was Rafik. She had stabbed
him multiple times and killed him. I
immediately felt relieved but I felt like I
was in the Twilight Zone. They told me that
she would be held and nothing would really
be done until Monday morning, and they

assured me that her family had been contacted.

I was delivered home around 7:30 a.m. I was exhausted and tried to lie down but I just looked at the ceiling and wondered what the hell went on down in that apartment while I was sleeping. I called Teddy at 10 a.m. and explained to him what had gone on, he was shocked. I told Teddy that I was getting off of the phone so that I could get dressed, I was going to go to the singing contest, it would be good to take my mind off of the drama. He said he would call me later to check on me.

I pulled up to the new church, it was really a gorgeous church, and it was packed, I'm sure Mt. Bentley would make out well with this turn out. The first person I saw when I entered was Kyle, he ran right up to me and said, "Edwin can I talk to you for a minute?" I said, "Sure Kyle, what's going on." He said, "First off, I'm nervous, I'm doing a solo for the competition." I said, "You do solos all the time, what's the issue?" He replied, "I'm not worried about anybody here except for this one queen that's here." I said, "Now Kyle why are you calling that young man that." He said, "Because she is, look at her – all the boys are all in her face with her sparkly ass shirt." I glanced over and I immediately understood where the insecurities were stemming from. I looked at what has to be the most gorgeous man I have ever seen, he stood about 5 foot 6 inches tall, his features were as pronounced as any model you've ever laid your eyes on and skin as smooth as any woman airbrushed in a magazine. His body was put together perfectly in all the right places to the point you noticed it with clothing on – ultra-flat stomach and perky round behind. The only way to describe him was pretty, and I mean so pretty that he almost didn't look real, like a living mannequin. I had to break my stare, I said to Kyle, "What's his name?" He said with a snotty attitude tone, "Topaz." I said, "Topaz, is that a stage name?" He said, "No, that's his real name, Topaz Jesper. He is here with his mom and dad, and his boyfriend's parents and brother. He is representing some church near the Philadelphia area, and I hear he can really blow." I said, "Well okay, the proper thing to do is to go over and introduce yourself, he may actually be a really nice person and all this anxiety will go away – you are a very talented singer and you know that; that is the only thing that you need to be worried about, you go up and do what you do and represent Mt. Bentley the best you can. Unless your hang up is deeper – you aren't intimidated by something other than his singing ability are you?" Kyle just gave me a look and said, "I ain't worried about that Bitch, this is my territory." I said, "Just as I thought, boy you are not even old enough to claim territory; let that mess go – you are in high school, I'm sure he is in college – there is no competition, and you said he's here with his boyfriend's family – ding, ding, ding he has a boyfriend, end of story." Kyle said, "No it's not the end of the story, the boyfriend was murdered about four months ago, so she is a threat." I said, "I'm done with this, you heard what I said, go introduce yourself and then take your lil' butt up there and sing, and slow your role." He rolled his eyes up in his head and said, "Okay."

As he made his way over to the young man that was causing him all the anxiety, I noticed Pastor Kareem off to the side and his eyes were fixed on the same person, I thought he was going to start drooling. I just shook my head and said to myself, 'What a mess!'

The competition got started right on time and singer after singer it just got better and better. Two acts before Kyle was to go on he ran over to me and said, "You were right Edwin, Topaz is so cool. He was showing me some different techniques to warm up my vocal chords. I feel bad for calling him a Bitch. We exchanged numbers and we are gonna keep in touch. He sings right after me, can you make sure you get a picture of us together and maybe we can be in your magazine, that would be the tea." He was genuinely happy to have made a new friend, I think it was the first time I ever seen him act his age. I gave myself a pat on the back and said, "Sure thing man, I'm

proud of you, you did the right thing, and
see what happened, we'll take a bunch of
pictures if you want when this is over."

I sat back and watched as it was Kyle's
turn up, he took center of the pulpit with
no nerves and went right into belting out
his song. He was by far the best act that
had come up so far, he really sang his heart
out. His upper register was always very
impressive for a male and he had the crowd
really up as he sang the lyrics…

Yet, Still I rise
Never to give up
Never to give in
Against all odds.

The whole time he was singing I could
see his new friend Topaz right down front
edging him on and clapping at his vocal
dynamics. You could see that the positive
reinforcement was doing wonders for Kyle's
performance, unlike the strange glares that
he usually receives on Sundays from some of
the shadier choir members and church members
who are really wrecked with jealousy – Kyle
is clearly the best singer that Mt. Bentley

has. Which is why he was given the solo for
this competition so that the prize money
could come back to Mt. Bentley, shady
business as usual. Mt. Bentley was giving
the function surely they shouldn't be able
to compete, but that's how they operate.

As Kyle ended his song on his knees
holding an impressively long note the crowd
was on their feet. You could tell in his
face that he was shocked and pleased with
the response. Topaz ran right out from the
audience and grabbed Kyle in a
congratulatory embrace. The two of them
walked back to the pews hand in hand like
they had been best friends forever, all of
Topaz's family greeted him with hugs and
congrats. While as usual Kyle's family
members blended into the background like the
child hadn't done anything, it was sad. He
found eye contact with me in the crowd and I
gave him a thumbs up. Next up was Topaz,
and from the hush and the whispers you could
tell this was the performance they were
waiting for. The lights of the church
glistened like new money off of his almost
see-thru black shirt that was covered with a

scatter of tiny rhinestones and the collar
and cuffs were completely covered in stones,
it was a beautiful sight accompanied with
his black perfectly fitted slacks and
Kenneth Cole loafers. There were four heavy
set sisters from his church standing behind
him quietly in solid black dresses with
rhinestones on the collars. He started his
song with no music, you could hear a pin
drop on carpet in the church when he opened
his mouth and out came the voice of an
absolute angel…

God has not promised me, sunshine
That's not the way it's going to be
But a little rain
Mixed with God's sunshine.
A little pain,
Makes me appreciate the good times.

Just then the female background joined in…

Be grateful
Be grateful

Then the band joined in and at that time the
whole church was already standing. Topaz
continued as the church flew off the handle
folks were shouting, and hollering out as he
got to the end of his song...

God said he would never

He motioned for the band to drop out,

Did you hear what I said church,
I said God said he would never

And then in a note reminiscent of only
Mariah Carey, Minnie Ripperton, Philip
Bailey or one of the DeBarge boys...

Never----------------

And he dropped his head as the church went
into a complete chaos for about two minutes,
he then lifted his head, held his hand up to
the heavens and with a single tear running
down his cheek he sang...

Never forsake you,

Be Grateful.

The church went crazy into praise for at
least ten minutes before Pastor Pearline
DiPuu could restore order. I did see her
speaking to Pastor Kareem before she took to
the microphone and they had strange looks
between the two of them. I was thinking,
'Oh geez, what now!'

Pastor DiPuu began, "Saints I beg you,
let's not be taken down by Satan's tricks!
He can cloud your judgment, and make you
feel for things that you know are not
natural. Men in sparkly blouses and singing
in a key higher than any woman in the church
- it's just wrong I tell you. And you need
not let the Devil have his way on today! I
beggeth you!!!!!" Well almost immediately
as the words escaped her mouth Topaz's
mother and his boyfriend's mother were down
at the pulpit with words for Pastor DiPuu.
Mrs. Jesper started, "How dare you, how dare
you judge my son - we did not come all this
way for this kind of foolishness, or to have
you down talk my child." Pastor DiPuu
didn't back down, she said, "Well you call

yourself women of God, you should've known not to present a decent church with the Devil's Spawn." Before she could say another word Topaz's boyfriend's mom yelled out, "Forgive me Lord but I can't do this today, forgive me my Savior!" and with the force of a mack truck she slapped Pastor DiPuu's face knocking her backwards and onto the ground. The scene was broken up immediately and they helped the pastor to her feet and sat her in a seat in the pulpit and gave her ice for her face, which was swelling fast. They sat the Jespers and the Rudolphsons in the pews and Pastor Kareem took to the pulpit.

He began, "Church it saddens me on today, that such a positive event has gone this way. And we have guests that are here from other church homes, I am especially not happy with my members as they know we do not uphold a spirit of homosexuality. And that is exactly what was going on here, I felt a spirit of faggotry moving throughout my church, let me tell you something – NOT IN HERE!!!!! I will not have it in here. Y'all are supposed to be singing to the glory of the Lord and what we got was men hugging each other like they are girlfriends meeting in a mall, men screaming and hollering at the top of their lungs thinking they are Mariah Carey. Those of you who did these things know who you are. The prize monies for today will not be given, I appreciate all of those who participated, but the high spirit of Lucifer has taken over and I will not distribute money, which is the root of all evil while that spirit is in my midst. Now as for my Mt. Bentley members, I have two members that I would like to come down front, Trevor and Kyle." I felt an emptiness in my stomach as the two teenagers came forth, I just knew something ugly was getting ready to happen.

The two of them stood facing Pastor Kareem as he started back into his rant, "We are only going to go over this once, this is not going to go on in here, NOT IN HERE!!!!! Men were made for women and women for men, period. My father used to say Adam and Eve, never Adam and Steve. You two are young men, not girls and if you don't understand that we can get some counseling going to

clear your mind from the confusion that is
HOMOSEXUALITY!!!!!! Men and women were
placed on the Earth by God to procreate –
how is that possible with two men, just look
at it, it's like a puzzle the pieces do not
fit! Two niggas hugged up ain't helpin'
nobody. Yes I can say it in slang too, as
long as you get what I'm saying. And
remember this, spit and shit don't make no
baby!!!!!!"

I almost fell over onto the floor, you
could hear the gasp in the room when that
last line fell from his lips. He continued
on, "You two will no longer be a part of Mt.
Bentley's choir as of this moment, and I
will let you know when and if the time comes
that you can participate again, now kindly
have a seat in the pews." Trevor broke into
tears of embarrassment and hurt as he took a
seat. Kyle literally stormed out of the
church and Topaz's whole group of family
members followed him and so did I. Once we
were outside I could see that Kyle was now
in tears, but Mrs. Jesper and Mrs.
Rudolphson were doing a great job at calming
him down. I introduced myself and told them

how much I appreciated all that had been
done for Kyle on this day by their family.
Mrs. Jesper said, "We are leaving this place
but please feel free to contact us anytime,
you all will have to come up and visit us,
we'd love to have you. And Edwin please
keep lifting this young man up, everybody
needs someone in their corner. And Kyle be
good to Edwin he is here for you." A few
seconds later three members of Kyle's family
approached the group of us, it was his
mother, his sister and his brother and you
could tell they were not happy. His mom
spoke out, "C'mon here, you done embarrassed
our whole family again, as usual. I'm ready
to go, I'm so sick of you and everything
about you!" Mrs. Rudolphson said, "How can
you feel that way about your own child, he
is not an embarrassment, he is a talented
young man, with the potential to really make
something of himself, but you must support
him." His mother replied, "You keep raising
yours and stay up outta my business, okay.
Kyle bring your faggot ass on!!!!!" We all
just stood in awe realizing there was

nothing that we could do to help him at this
time, it was a very painful moment for me.

I walked Topaz and his family members
to their cars and seen them off and then I
started back into the church, it was high
time that Pastor Kareem and I have a little
chat. As I got into the sanctuary I spotted
him, I walked over to him and said, "Hey
Pastor Kareem can I have a moment to speak
with you please?" He said, "Sure, and how's
my article coming?" We started walking
toward his office; I noticed that his two
henchmen were coming as well. I said,
"That's part of what I want to talk about,
but I only want you, I don't want to speak
with them, just you." He said, "Okay," and
shooed them off and he and I went into the
office. He said, "Have a seat Sir." I sat
down as he went over to the other side of
his desk and sat down; he said, "So how is
the article coming?" I said, "Well that is
part of what I want to talk about, but let
me start first by saying — as a person who
is considering joining Mt. Bentley, today I
was appalled." A look of confusion occupied
his face. I continued, "I found that whole

fiasco about homosexuality and the way that the singing was done was so unnecessary. And to call those two kids out and embarrass them in front of all those people – how could you do that?" The look of confusion was now replaced with disdain, as he replied, "There could only be one reason that you feel so strongly about that and that is you must be wracked with the spirit of homosexuality yourself, and the guilt has you here now seeking to have your soul freed!" I looked at him with an intense eye contact and said, "Man, are you serious? Quit your playing. Have you honestly forgotten where and when we first met?" He said, "Do tell…"

I said, "Fine then, let's play your little game Kareem or should I call you Shakeem, being as though that's what you told me your name was. Is it coming back to you now, Gay Pride D.C. a few years ago, a good night of activity but no return calls, it was cool though."

I could see the anger boiling over, it was showing all over his face.

I kept going, "My point is, you are a grown man, do whatever you choose and keep your secrets, but what you did today was ridiculously hypocritical – if you are closeted, you just shouldn't preach on the subject at all, and you definitely never put anyone else on blast – not cool, not cool at all!"

He sat back very arrogantly in his chair and said, "So is it that I never called you back that has you so upset? I gave you the dick faggot, what more did you want?" I chuckled at him and said, "Really you little closet freak, let me refresh your memory, it was an even exchange – I still remember the look of satisfaction all over your face when my nine and a half inches capped off deep up in yo' guts partner. You squealed just like one of those lil' sanctified cunts that you spoke of this afternoon so drop the hard act – sweet bottoms." He jumped up from his chair and yelled, "I'll have your ass kicked!" I said, "For real, that seems a little harsh, how bout I take and bend you over in here and make your ass pulsate again, that seems

143

to calm your nerves a bit. All you have to
do is ask reverend, cause you do have some
good ass!" He said, "Get out of my church!"
I said, "Gladly, because all the sins being
committed here are a good indication as to
why the former church burned completely to
the ground, and the lightning bolt won't be
long hitting this one, I just hope that this
time you are in here when it burns. And
another thing, don't think anyone is fooled
by how you swindled and kept that money
today, you depended on Kyle winning but you
knew that Topaz's performance was a sure win
– so that whole lil bit with you and Pastor
DiPuu, your fellow ass clown was all a put
on for Mt. Bentley to keep the money, people
aren't as stupid as you think they are.
Trust me, I thought I would get something
positive to say in an article today and it
turned out like all the rest of the research
I've done on Mt. Bentley – shifty and shady!
There's not enough good things to write a
whole article to make you or your church
look good. Now I have enough dirt to write
an excellent page turning article, but you
will be left standing in your truth, and you

aren't looking so good!" He said, "Get the fuck out and I mean now – and if you print one thing in that magazine I will sue until there isn't a magazine anymore!" I said, "Awwww, are ya gonna take me to the court for undercover bible-toting cocksuckers who live a constant lie, well praise God!" He said, "You have two seconds and I swear, I'm gonna have you fucked up, you Bitch!" I said, "Okay, I'm going, and rest your heels for now queen; a story like yours deserves a much wider audience than my little magazine. You take care of yourself pastor and - Oh yeah, see you in court!" I burst into laughter as I exited his office.

Chapter Ten
"Standing In Your Truth"

Three months had gone by since I had seen Miranda, and I had butterflies in my stomach on this morning, the morning of her trial for killing Rafik. I haven't been permitted to see her because I am being called to testify, it really sucks, I miss her and have been really worried about her. Her family has been really nice in keeping me informed of her well being, and they are all here in Pittsburgh, they had a caravan of about thirty folks that drove down from New Orleans for the trial today. My brother Teddy also drove in from Maryland to be with me, and having Teddy around always makes things easier for me.

Today is also a big day for me, it is the release date of my new book. I told my publisher that I had to go to court but I will be able to get text messages for any news. On the way to court Teddy and I discussed the book, he was laughing at all of the crazy things that were in the book, I always send him an advance manuscript before I release anything, he said he absolutely loved it. Then he said to me, "I am a lil' nervous though Eddie Jimmy, what's gonna happen if that bastard really does try to sue you?" I said, "Oh trust me he is a money hound, so he will definitely try to sue, but I released the book as a work of fiction, I changed some things and changed all the names and places so he will lose the case, but it will be nice to see him tell his own truth by trying to fight, it is like an admission of guilt – what an asshole! But he is going to burn in hell chasing after a five dollar bill, he is just greedy!" We laughed as we parked the car in Macy's Parking Lot, I said, "If this all turns out well, I'm gonna stop back through here and buy Miranda something nice, I know she is sick of that jumpsuit – you know how she is." Teddy laughed and said, "I know how you both are, way too much alike, even the same taste in men." I said, "You shut your mouth, she doesn't know about that and I will take it to my grave, that would hurt her and I will not do that, ever."

As we took our seat it was refreshing to see all the familiar faces from Mt. Bentley that showed up to support Miranda, including Pastor Kareem, I hadn't seen him since our little argument. It seems that Rafik really did have a pretty large family and a lot of them showed up as well. Once court got started it was pretty intense, as soon as they brought Miranda in you could hear the unrest of Rafik's family members, at the sight of her tears began to run down my face. She was crying as well when she saw the outpouring of support for her in the courtroom.

I was called to the stand pretty early on for questioning. It wasn't really too bad, I just told that I knew he and Miranda had a thing going on since right after I moved to town and that I'd seen him coming and going from her place frequently over the last few months. And then I told the story of him dragging her from the church and how forceful he was and when I stepped in how he beat me up. I hated to tell that part, because I never told Teddy about that and as I went back to my seat I could see the anger in his face. He said, "Oh we will talk, I told you that I would hurt him," I said, "Shhh, I know Teddy, that's why I didn't say anything." Next was the moment of truth, it was what I had been waiting for all these months. What happened in that apartment while I was sleeping right upstairs.

Miranda took the stand and they asked her to explain what happened on the night that she killed Rafik. She took a deep breath and she started, "I was having wine and listening to music with Edwin when Rafik came to the door. Edwin told me not to answer him but I didn't listen, Edwin didn't want to have anything to do with Rafik after the fight at the church so he left. Rafik came into the apartment and it was cool at first and then he started up with his mood swings and asking me for some money. I told him that I didn't appreciate nor would I contribute to what had now become a bad habit."

Rafik's lawyer interrupted her, "And what habit would that be Ms. Morand?" She continued, "He had become a crack addict!" The lawyer yelled out, "That's heresay!" The judge said, "Overruled, crack-cocaine was found in his system, it is stated in the toxicology report, continue Ms. Morand."

She cleared her throat and continued, "From there the argument just got worse, he started in on me about my pastor. He kept saying, 'You fucking whore, get some money from the church.' I kept telling him he was crazy but he wouldn't let it go. This was not the first time that he brought it up, he had devised a whole plan of how I was going to blackmail my pastor. I maintained that I would never deal in any way like that." The lawyer broke in again and said, "Ms. Moran, who is your pastor and is he here today?" She responded, "Pastor Kareem Bentley and yes he is present in the courtroom." He responded, "Were you or had you at anytime carried on an affair with this pastor?" She sat quietly for a few moments, the judge said, "Answer the question please." She said, "I am so sorry, yes I have." You could hear gasps and chatter throughout the courtroom, the judge slammed his gavel and said, "Order." Miranda started back on her testimony, "It was about 12:30 a.m. and I asked Rafik to leave, and he wouldn't - he just started screaming, 'You fuckin' dat nigga and can't get a penny out of him, you truly are useless.' I told him that was it, I had enough and to get his ass out of my house, he yelled back, 'Fuck you Bitch, I'll go when I'm ready.' I then told him I was going to call the police and have him removed. I reached over and grabbed my cordless phone, he snatched the phone off of me and hit me in the nose with it two times and you can see in my xrays he broke my nose in two places between the beating with the phone and the repeated punches that followed. I tried to run but he grabbed me by my hair and slammed me backwards on top of my glass coffee table, the glass shattered and cut my legs in six places, and multiple ones on my back as well. He then drug me by my hair to the kitchen and the whole time he kept telling me he was going to slit my throat…"

She broke down into tears as she continued, "his eyes were dancing in his head and it was like I didn't see Rafik anymore, I just saw a madman. And I knew I had to fight for my life. He took me and slammed my head against the counter by the sink repeatedly, I lost track of how many times my head was slammed against it; I felt like I was going to black out until I seen the blade of the knife glistening in the light. I felt him stab me in my shoulder twice and after that my body was numb, I didn't even feel the knife cutting my hands as I struggled to get it off of him. He still had my hair with one hand and as we tussled he dropped the knife. When he bent over to pick it up, I lunged into his crotch with my head and bit into it, he had on sweatpants so I was able to get a good bite and I locked down on him until he screamed out. Then I grabbed the knife and I stabbed him until he stopped moving. I called the police and told them what happened and I sat there with the knife until they arrived, I really didn't know he was dead, I wouldn't even take my eyes off of him until I heard the police, they actually had to kick in the door because I was to scared to go and open it." The lawyer said, "So your telling the court that you stabbed him until he stopped moving; Ms. Morand are you saying it took you to stab him twenty-seven times before he stopped moving?" She responded, "Sir have you ever been in a fight for your life?" He said, "Objection, I don't see the relevance of her question." Miranda said, "The relevance is – would you have been counting or cutting – me, I kept cutting!" He said, "No further questions your honor, I believe she is a cold blooded killer!" The judge said, "Watch it, I didn't ask you for a judgment call!" He said, "I apologize your honor." The judge then asked, "Is there anything further you would like to share Ms. Morand?"

Miranda sat up straight in her chair and said, "Yes Sir. I have to be very honest here, not because I'm under oath, but because I know it is wrong to take a life. I had no other choice in the matter, one of us was not going to walk away from this. But what I have to be honest about is, up until last week I was having a hard time sleeping, all I see when I close my eyes is visions of Rafik and the good times we had and then him laying in a pool of blood. The images were haunting me. Then last week I went to have a physical done and I found out that I am HIV positive and the virus was also found in his toxicology report. So you see, I don't have the nightmares anymore and I don't feel as bad as I did at first for killing Rafik, because he killed me first." And with that she dropped her head. You could hear a pin drop in that courtroom.

The judge called for a one hour recess, and the silence never broke as the courtroom cleared out. After checking on Miranda's family Teddy and I decided to go grab a bite to eat at Primanti Bros sandwich shop in the base of Macy's parking lot, I had been telling Teddy about their famous Rueben sandwiches. On the walk over to the restaurant Teddy asked, "How's your health lil' man?" I said, "Teddy I'm cool, my last test was a week ago and I was negative and of course I will keep getting tested, but I have never done any sexual act unprotected with Rafik, I'm confident that I'm cool." He said, "You better be, Ewwww! I could dig that nigga up and kill him again, I told you I just got a bad feeling about that dude just from the first time you mentioned him." I said, "And speaking of, you came in contact with Miranda." He said, "I've been tested since then, but I'm going to get another one, but it was just head, but you can't be too careful. I hope she gets off, she shouldn't have to serve any time for a piece of shit dude like this." Just then I got a text message from my publisher that said, 'Grab a NY Times!'

We grabbed one on the way back up to the courthouse and there it was as big as day…

Between Pews by *Edwin James*
debuting #2 on New York Times Bestseller List

I was ecstatic, but the celebration was cut short, the butterflies remained in my stomach for my friend as we entered the Court House. We got back in the courtroom and took our seats. Both lawyers gave closing statements, Miranda's lawyer went first.

She stood and said, "To this court today I have presented my client, in this classic case of a woman who fell for a guy who took the wrong road in life and when she wouldn't follow along he turned on her, but in this situation he turned to a rage and tried to take her life. She fought back and made it out alive. Is that a crime? I don't think so; the only crime here is that

she didn't come out unharmed. She came out
with a life sentence that not even this
court could appoint; a life as a person
living with the HIV virus. I believe my
client is innocent and in no way deserves to
serve two life sentences at the hands of the
same attacker. Thank you.

Next was Rafik's lawyer, "Today we have
seen a woman who had multiple sex partners
and got tangled up in her own web of deceit.
She knew that my client was a bit of a hot
head, a bad boy if you will. But she
willingly engaged in the physicality that
brought them to this point, their fights
just got worse and worse. The authorities
were never contacted which says to me that
she was a willing participant and this time
things got out of hand. And when she saw
the opportunity she killed my client in cold
blood. She used excessive force to kill,
not to stop the attack but to kill! Thank
you.

We sat as the judge went back in his
quarters for about thirty minutes, and when
he came back he said, "I'm ready to rule…"

"In the case of Rafik Jerry vs. Miranda Morand, I find the defendant Miranda Morand… Not Guilty due to Self-defense, and temporary insanity."

Cheers erupted in the courtroom, such relief was felt. But on the other side it was just the opposite for Rafik's family. It was odd, because actually there were no winners and when it comes to murder, there never is.

As Teddy and I stood for a moment collecting our thoughts on the front steps of the courthouse up walks Pastor Kareem and his two goons. He arrogantly said, "This was a good day in court for our sister. You might as well get ready for your day, I don't think your verdict will be so favorable." Teddy erupted, "Man go head wit' dat' bullshit!" I said, "No Teddy it's okay, I will see you in whatever court you would like to see me in." He replied, "I hope you sell enough of your little books, cause it's gonna cost you!" I said, "Oh you didn't hear, your getting all the publicity that you asked for, grab a New York Times, I got you that wide audience I promised, the book debuted at number two, so I'm sure the coins will be lovely, but how will yours hold up, or will you set fire to your new church to sustain your lifestyle. But you have bigger fish to fry don't you? You need to go be tested and see if you can save your marriage. Your wasting time talking to me and who knows; your days may be numbered kind Sir. From where I sit, I think I'm winning and hell you've given me more than enough material to write a sequel, you and your antics are going to make me a very rich man." He just stood there gritting his teeth and said, "Fuck you, faggot!"

I laughed and said, "Fuck me, what are you trying to do Pastor, kill me? Trust me you and I will not get together, not even on your best day; how ever many that is, that you have left. Good luck to ya!"

<u>THE END</u>

For more from James Colwell
Also read...

Loving Topaz

Losing Topaz

Learning Topaz

CPSIA information can be obtained
at www.ICGtesting.com
Printed in the USA
BVHW041714050820
585602BV00008B/180